My Bitch, Yo Bitch.....Everybody Bitch

-A Novel Written by-

Niki Jilvontae

Copyright © 2014 by True Glory Publications

Published by True Glory Publications LLC

Join our Mailing list by texting TrueGlory at 95577

Facebook: Author Niki Jilvontae

This novel is a work of fiction. Any resemblances to actual events, real people, living or dead, organizations, establishments or locales are products of the author's imagination. Other names, characters, places, and incidents are used fictitiously.

Cover Design: Michael Horne

Editor: Kylar Bradshaw

Because of the dynamic nature of the Internet, any Web addresses or links contained in this book may have changed since publication, and may no longer be valid. The views

D1714125

expressed in this work are solely those of the author and do not necessarily reflect the views of the publisher and the publisher hereby disclaims any responsibility for them.

Dedications

This book is dedicated to all of the sneaky, lying, side pieces—Everywhere!! Be careful because your actions may catch up with you…

Acknowledgements

First and foremost, I'd like to thank The Most High for giving me this amazing gift and allowing me to share it with the world. I'd also like to thank my literary sisters and brothers who always keep me encouraged and focused on the big picture. I would also like to thank the following very special family, friends, and supporters: J-mauel Starnes, Daphne BlackDiamond Woodland, Tera L.Kirksey-Coleman, Prisciilla Payton, Cheryl

Hines, Tameka Cameron, Real Alwaysaqueen Divas, Jennifer Stephens, Courtney Matthews, Crystal Sullivan, Wendy Gettsum Cox, Kylar Bradshaw (my beautiful editor), Lawanda Lovie Hulett, Mileta Young Timmons, Raven Perkins, Victorious Johnson, Jr., Cole B. Hicks, Monica Parker, Candyann Ferris, Varski Moore, Authoress Michele V. Mitchell, Chandra Davis, Latoya MsParker Mc Farland, Jomara Rogers, Antonio D. Lauderdale, KFarrell Peoples, Ebony Shamone Sayles, Rolls Ross, and Lynn Lewis. Thank you all for the encouragement, love, and support. I really appreciate it!! <3 Niki Jilvontae

Table of Contents

My Bitch, Yo Bitch....
EVERYBODY BITCH!!

Written By:

Niki Jilvontae

Part 1

The text that started it all!!!

Chapter 1

Mike

"Bzzzzzzz! Bzzzzzzz!"

The nightstand next to the bed came to life. Over and over again, LiLi's phone went off. I tried to ignore it, but that muthafucka wouldn't stop. Text after text, that shit was driving me insane. I turned my head towards the nightstand and looked at the clock....3:27 a.m.? '*Who the fuck texting*

LiLi, my wife at 3 in the morning?' I thought to myself as I glanced over at her thick ass lying naked next to me. I was so in love with her smooth cocoa skin and that fat ghetto ass. She had me hypnotized by her big brown eyes... that long black hair...and her smell!!!

Damn my bitch was fine and I loved the shit out of her, but that was irrelevant at the moment. The fact was, I couldn't trust that bitch. Hell after all the shit she had put me through, I shouldn't and probably never would trust any other bitch.

I quickly grabbed LiLi's phone off the nightstand and palmed it like a ghetto kid who found a dollar on the street. Happy as fuck to finally have the opportunity to get my hands on her damn phone, I jumped my ass up and went into the bathroom. After closing and locking the door behind me, I began my investigation.

"Damn, what's her lock code?" I whispered to myself as I sat down on the toilet and tried to figure it out.

I entered 0206, the month and year we met, into the phone...... Access Denied.

"DAMN!!" I mumbled to myself as I felt my anger start to build.

'What the fuck is the code?' I thought as I continued entering numbers into the phone like 0407...1211, neither worked. I entered all five of the kid's birthdays, old addresses...everything, but nothing worked.

"This bitch slick." I said to myself.

By then my patience was beginning to run thin, so I started entering random numbers hoping I would get lucky. That shit was taking forever;

because after three wrong tries, I had to wait one minute before I could try again. Twenty tries later and still no entry.

"What the fuck?" I mumbled as I felt my frustration and anger rising to the point of being pissed.

I started pacing back and forth, looking at myself in the mirror as beads of sweat dripped down my bald head and across the folds in my forehead. For a second I noticed my eyes....I saw the rage. I looked like a fucking rabbit-dog....crazy.

Only LiLi could have that effect on me. The thought of her fucking another nigga drove me crazy. Hell, she already had three kids on me when I was locked up, so in my eyes she was capable of any fucking thing. I wasn't gone but two lil' funky ass years, and that bitch couldn't wait on me. She had our twins, Montae and Allanna, by this nigga named Marco in December 2008 just seven months after I got locked up. That and the fact that she already had a tarnished reputation in the hood. Proving to me that while I was gone away doing time, she was fucking off.

Yea, LiLi did one of the worse things a female could do to her man in jail. As if Montae and Allanna weren't enough to push a nigga over the edge, LiLi had another child. Our son, Myles, by some random ass nigga in November 2009. So imagine my surprise when I got out in 2010 and had four kids waiting on me, instead of one. I guess our own daughter, Alaya, who was born April 2007 wasn't enough for her. I guess the bitch wanted a baby by every fucking body. ..

After all of that, I still forgave her and vowed to be the man my father never was. I could never leave my children in the world to fend for themselves like my dad did my brother and me when we were little. He left two men to be raised by a woman, and a woman to bare all of the weight of the world alone. I resented him for a long time for leaving us with no warning or justification. That shit made a nigga bitter and angry as fuck for a while, lashing out at everyone who tried to get close to me. That all changed when I got locked up though.

When I went to jail, I realized that I was being to my daughter, Alaya, exactly who my father was to me and I didn't want her to know that type of pain. I wanted better for her and in order for me to offer her better, I knew that I had to work on myself. I spent 25 months, 1 week, 3 days, 9 hours, 41 minutes, and 17 seconds behind concrete walls determined to be a better me for my daughter. After that, I got out and never looked back. I came my ass home, got my shit together, and took care of my family. I won't lie, I was hurt like a muthafucka when I first found out about the other kids. However, after seeing their faces, I couldn't deny the love I felt. I loved all my kids, all of them were mine regardless. My kids were my number one priority and I valued the concept of family more than anything.

Despite the hurt, anger, and nagging feeling of betrayal I carried around in my heart after meeting my three new children, I forgave LiLi and she had MY son, Michael Jr., December 2011. The day my son, Mikey, was born was one of the happiest days of my life, watching LiLi have my daughter Alaya was the other. I can still remember the love and pride I felt as I held him in my arms. He was so big and alert, looking right into my eyes and smiling like he knew who I was. I couldn't hold back my tears looking at my son, my legacy smiling back at me. I think that was when I looked at LiLi and decided I would love her forever.

She had given me two of the greatest gifts a person could receive. I was lucky enough to watch both of my children be born into the world and physically be there with them each day to see them learn and grow. Maine that was a gift that was priceless to me. LiLi had given me something no one else ever could, my first son and daughter. Those gifts LiLi gave me helped to create a bond between her and I that was unbreakable.

I would love LiLi forever if she let me and she knew it. However, all of the love, admiration, and gratitude I felt for LiLi couldn't change the fact that she had cheated many times before. It was those hoeish ways of hers that always seem to creep into the picture and kept me on edge. I could never truly be fucking happy and live in the moment because I knew at any moment, LiLi could do something to mess it all up. It was like if things were going really good for us, she couldn't rest. She just had to do something to stir up shit and cause friction.

I guess LiLi craved excitement, while I on the other hand just wanted to be happy. I didn't need all of the materialistic bullshit, status, and the fast pace lifestyle that LiLi craved. All I needed was the kids, her, food, shelter, clothing...and love. Those things along with trust were enough for me, but not for LiLi though. She was never really satisfied with anything I did or anything the world gave her for that matter, which is why she seemed to enjoy making other's lives miserable. Almost every heartache or argument we had ever gone through was her fault because she wanted something she didn't have. That's why I had to see who was texting her.

I entered 0508 into the phone's keypad. Suddenly, the phone unlocked and LiLi's home screen appeared, revealing a picture of some athlete nigga with no shirt on. I shook my head and sucked my teeth at that bullshit. I wasn't sweating that nigga she'd never even meet. I was more worried about what nigga she could possibly be fucking right under my nose. For some reason, I couldn't stop wondering why 0508 was her lock code. That was the month and year I went to jail.

"What the bitch do celebrate that day or some shit?" I asked myself out loud as I pushed the message icon on her android.

As soon as the picture message loaded, I damn near put my fist through the wall. The shit I saw in LiLi's phone was something any man would be livid over finding.

"Some nigga sending MY BITCH a picture of his dick at 3 o'clock in the fucking morning. Some white muthafucka at that. What the fuck?" I yelled to myself.

I watched as my hands started shaking like a muthafucka, but I tried to keep control as I scrolled down and read the attached text: *Baby, I'm waiting!!! :-)*

That was the straw that broke the camel's back. Someone was about to get their ass kicked. I wanted to know who the fuck that nigga was calling MY baby and what the fuck he THOUGHT he was waiting for.

I stormed out of the bathroom with LiLi's phone in my hand, flicking on every fucking light on my way to our bed.

"LiLi....LiLi. Maine, you hear me!" I said mushing her head into the pillow.

"WAKE-THE-FUCK- UPPP!!" I yelled as I stood over her sexy, drunk ass lying there in a damn coma.

I knew she heard me calling her name and felt that damn mush, but her ass didn't move. She knew I was mad as hell and she was probably mad at herself for leaving her phone out the night before. That's what her wonna-be slick ass got.

"LiLi...wake yo ass up and explain this shit!" I yelled throwing her cell phone on the bed.

Finally after a few more seconds, LiLi started moving.

"Damn bae, what?" She asked me sitting up and wiping the sleep out of her big brown eyes. "What the fuck is you hollering at 3 o'clock in the morning for Mike?" LiLi yelled at me after quickly looking at the clock on the nightstand.

The nerve of this bitch! Some nigga was texting her dick pictures at 3 a.m., but she was hollering at me for waking her up? She had obviously lost her fucking mind. I had to stop myself from slapping her ass out of the bed by closing my eyes and counting to ten, remembering my anger management techniques. I really needed them at that moment too because I could've beaten the shit out of her right then. I could feel that blind rage I felt the day I caught the charge that sent me to jail as I stared down at LiLi. I wanted to shake the shit out of her sitting there doe-eyed and shit, but I loved her too much to do that.

Regardless of how bad she treated me, she was my everything. At the same time though, my pride wouldn't let me just sit back and let LiLi's deceitful ass play me. I didn't want to hit her though....I'd probably kill her if I did. Her 5'6" and 165 lb. frame was no match for my 6'3" and 237 lb. of pure muscle and anger. I probably would've broke her little ass in half, but that's what I felt like doing if she didn't hurry up and tell me what the fuck was going on.

"Huh?" LiLi asked me with a scared look on her face as she picked up her phone, unlocked it, and looked at the text message then back up at me.

I know I must've looked like a monster standing there with sweat all over me and my fists clenched because LiLi instantly started crying and pleading her case.

"Mike...no baby. This text isn't even for me. My friend Tasha gave a dude my number so he wouldn't have to call her house. You know her mama don't play that and she don't have a cell." LiLi cried with big, innocent tear-filled eyes.

'Damn that bitch was convincing. She had her shit together.' I thought to myself. LiLi

14

continued to cry and plead, begging me not to leave her for no reason and telling me how much she loved me. I really didn't want to hear that shit though. I was fed up with all the lying and cheating shit and she could tell.

"Baby, please believe me." LiLi continued to beg.

I watched her through my rage with tears streaming down her face and I felt my heart begin to melt. She looked so sweet and innocent as she pleaded with me through her eyes. LiLi knew that she was my biggest weakness and loved to play on my soft heart for her. She knew how much I loved her with no limits, trusting most of what she said without questioning it. However, this time I had a gut feeling that the bitch was lying.

"Maine...fuck that shit. Why the fuck the Tasha bitch have to give the nigga yo number?

You got a mutha fucking husband now, LiLi! We been married a whole year so a muthafucka would think you'd know the rules by now. It's certain shit you just don't FUCKING DO!!" I yelled while putting my hands on my head to keep from choking her ass.

I had to pace the floor beside the bed and count to ten until my anger started to subside. The whirlwind of emotions LiLi was putting me through had me fighting an internal battle between killing her lying ass or continuing to love her and let her lie to me. That shit had a nigga so confused my head began to spin. I felt like she was driving me fucking crazy.

"Baby, watch this. I can prove it." LiLi said while sniffling and dialing the number from the text.

I stopped pacing and stood facing her with my arms folded as the call went through. Suddenly, a white dude answered the phone on the first ring, igniting jealousy and malice I tried to keep buried inside.

"What's up baby?" The white dude said after answering the phone and I lost my fucking mind.

I couldn't believe some random muthafucka had the audacity to call my bitch his baby after all I had done for her. I was the muthafucka who had sacrificed his entire life for her. I went to jail for beating a nigga because of HER. I did two whole years and still came home to her and children that weren't mine. Where the fuck was this white nigga when she needed help? He had me fucked up thinking he was going to come in and reap the benefits of my hard work. Hell no, that shit wasn't about to happen.

"What the fuck? Nigga, you ain't got no muthafucking babies over here!" I yelled as LiLi covered the phone with her hand.

I had to stare at myself in the mirror for a second to make sure shit was real when I saw LiLi cover the phone. I couldn't understand why that bitch thought I was a fool and she could play me like some trick. I felt like The Hulk as I watched myself transform into a monster in the mirror. Veins popped out of my neck and deep creases formed across my forehead as I began to yell and my body began to tremble in fury.

"What the fuck you covering the phone for LiLi?" I yelled as I snatched the phone out of her hand.

I glared at LiLi with hate in my eyes as she scooted back in the bed and tucked her legs underneath her while embracing herself. She tried not to meet my hateful glare as I continued to stare her down while yelling.

"Aye homeboy. Who the fuck is this and how do you know my wife?" I yelled into the phone while still staring at LiLi who had her eyes closed, and was humming and rocking back-and-forth gently.

I continued to look at LiLi with the most hateful glance I could produce while waiting on the nigga to respond. Rage surged through me like electricity as I listened to the bitch nigga on the other end of the line breathing. The anger that was in me was driving me to the point of insanity and a nervous breakdown just thinking that LiLi wasn't who she pretended to be. I felt like a little bitch all caught up in female feelings. However, I knew that I had to appear to be in control of my emotions at all times. Despite the fact that on the inside I felt like a lil' ass boy, I had to remain a real nigga.

It was bad enough I was even in this situation again. Once gain wondering whether or not LiLi was sharing herself with another man. You'd think I would have learned my lesson after all of the other times. How much bullshit could a nigga put up with before he just gave the fuck up? I was tired of having to watch and be aware all the damn time. Yet, there I was investigating a damn picture, while LiLi was once again crying and lying, and this bitch ass nigga held the phone and wouldn't say shit!

"Aye homeboy... WHO-THE-FUCK-ARE YOU?" I yelled again so loudly that LiLi covered her ears and looked on in terror.

She hadn't seen me that mad since we were kids. She knew my temper though, so she knew the situation was serious. She could see my frustration building the entire time as I stood there trembling with my heart on my sleeve feeling like a fucking fool. I was just about to throw her phone at her fucking head when the muthafucka on the other end of the phone began to talk.

"Oh, h.. hello." The muthafucka said stuttering. "My name is Stuart and I was texting for Tasha." He said in a tone just above a whisper.

At that moment, I realized the muthafucka calling my bitch was no more than a pussy and he was scared as fuck now that he had to face a real nigga. I almost forgot how serious the situation was and started laughing when I heard the muthafucka whimper into the phone like a wounded puppy. Stuart gasped for air and his voice trembled when he attempted to say a word. From the sound of his voice, I would have betted a million dollars that the nigga shitted on himself. I had to hold back my snicker as I thought about a grown man shitting on himself because he let another man scare him over the phone.

The thought of that shit had me amused to my core; however, there wasn't shit funny about that nigga texting my bitch. There wasn't anything funny about the entire situation and I couldn't feel sorry for either one of their asses either, no matter how much they cried and whimpered. I did kinda feel like a fool though since the bitch appeared to be telling the truth, but deep down something was telling me that both of their asses were lying. Despite those thoughts, I kept my shit together and continued my tirade.

"Well NIGGA, this ain't Tasha phone. This LiLi phone so don't call or text it no muthafucking more!" I yelled.

I was so mad I was damn near foaming at the mouth as I held LiLi's phone tightly in my hand and glared at her. I could hear the pussy's heart beating through the phone as I growled through clenched teeth. I bet his weak ass wouldn't call my bitch no more.

"You heard what I said Nigga?" I asked him while still yelling.

He managed a low toned, "Yes."

"If I ever see yo number in her phone again, I'm coming to break yo fucking neck pussy!!" I yelled before pressing the end button and erasing his text and number out of LiLi's phone, throwing it back on the bed.

"See baby, I told you." LiLi said sliding to the edge of the bed and grabbing me around my waist, laying her head on my stomach.

As soon as I felt the touch of her warm skin radiating through my shirt, electricity shot through my body. She had me hooked and it had been that way since we met in 2006 when I was sixteen. She was only fifteen so I thought that I would easily control her...make her MINE. However, she had an unbreakable hold on me from that first touch. It was the same at that moment...she had me. LiLi had me for life whether she wanted me or not.

"Baby, you are the only man for me. This is your pussy and only your pussy...believe me." LiLi said seductively.

My heart raced and I felt my dick jump in my boxer-briefs as LiLi pulled me closer and yanked my boxers down, kissing me down my stomach. That shit felt good as hell, but I couldn't be a bitch. I had to fight the urge to submit to her like I always did.

"Maine, go on LiLi." I said playing like I was resisting, but really that shit felt like life itself.

Just then, she grabbed my dick and put ALL of it in her mouth, balls deep. I think I died and came back to life twice as I stood there, knees buckling while she massaged my dick with her tongue.

"DAMMMNNN..... She got me again." I said to myself as I let my head fall back and LiLi took control.

LiLi's mouth was so wet and warm that my dick grew from about 5 inches on soft to 10 inches of solid power in seconds. She sucked me like a fucking porn star and I loved every minute of it. I loved her despite everything she took me through, but I wondered how long that love could keep her safe from the rage inside of me. That rage that

25

wanted her to face the consequences for her actions. That part of me that had to teach her to never play with a nigga's heart.

I looked deep into LiLi's deceitful eyes as she stared at me while licking up my shaft. Then she used the tip of her tongue to make circles around my dick head as she gently blew on it......then quickly deep throated it.

That shit almost made me shiver and my knees give out, but I kept it together. I held in my moans as she continued to deep throat my dick while spit and precum ran all down her chin, and she massaged my nuts while moaning. Maine, this shit felt so damn good, I couldn't even be mad at her anymore. I felt my body relax and that rage and hint of insanity inside of me disappear as LiLi gave me all of her. In that moment, I couldn't believe that my baby would cheat on me after sucking me like she did. She couldn't...at least I hoped she wouldn't because I might fucking kill her if she did.

Ignoring the thoughts running through my head, I pulled LiLi's hair while ramming my dick deeper and deeper down her throat. Her tongue did a full massage on my dick in fast, slippery flicks as I closed my eyes and bit my bottom lip. I felt my toes curl as she sucked me into ecstasy. I knew right then that it was going to be a damn good day at work. I couldn't help but shiver as I closed my eyes, put my head back, and bust all in LiLi's mouth. She looked at me seductively as cum ran from the corners of her mouth and she licked her fingers, drinking all of me. *'Damn, I love my bitch to death,'* is all I could think as she continued to suck me dry.

Chapter 2

<u>LiLi</u>

Mike must have lost his damn mind thinking I was going to let him catch me that easily. I had already told Stuart and all of my other tricks that if a nigga ever called them or answered my phone when they called, they should say they were calling for my best friend, Tasha. Hell, Tasha knew the game too. Mike's dumb ass just didn't know. His ass was so blinded by love he couldn't see the shit right in front of his face. Mike only saw what he wanted to see, and that's me loving him and him only. He thought the sun rose and set in my ass. In his eyes, I could do no wrong. That was before this picture.

I have to admit that I was worried that he was gone whoop my ass for a second. He was so fucking mad when he found that dick pic in my phone, but his anger didn't last long. This fye cap wins every time. I had the potion to put Mike in a trance whenever I needed him to be. I had his ass so blinded by love, good pussy, and fye head he would believe any fucking thing I said, even when he knew I was lying. I could feel that nigga's knees buckle from the very first time I deep throated his dick, confirming what I already thought--men were weak.

From that very first time I put my hands on Mike, I knew that I would have his hard ass wrapped around my finger. If he only knew all the shit I did on a daily basis, I wonder would he still love me as much if he knew. What he didn't know wouldn't hurt him though because I wasn't saying shit. As long as he kept paying the bills, taking care of the kids, and giving me what I wanted when I wanted it...I'd PLAY wifey. I'd keep my fucking mouth shut and play whatever role he wanted me to as long as he kept doing what I asked.

I still couldn't help but to wonder sometimes though, what he'd do to me if he knew about all the niggas I was fucking. Would he be the pussy he had become and kill himself? Or would he turn total psycho and kill me, then himself? I tried to imagine Mike's soft ass beating me or even killing me as I submerge my body down into the hot bubble bath he ran for me before he and the kids left. Although he had come home, the type of nigga I hated: possessive, needy, and always in his feelings. I had to admit he was still a damn good man and I didn't want to lose him or push him over the edge just yet. He always took good care of me and four kids that weren't his with no problem, even though he thought only three weren't his. I often wondered what he'd do if he ever found out our oldest child Alaya wasn't his either, just our youngest MJ was his.

"He'll probably kill my ass if he ever finds out." I said to myself while laughing and lowering my body deeper into the water. "He ain't gone do shit," I told myself.

Besides, that nigga thought he owned me, always had. I loved him and all for everything he had done for me, but I just didn't love him like he loved me anymore. He was too damn lame for me since he got out of jail and changed his life. All he wanted to ever do was have family time with me and the kids, and cuddle and shit. Fuck all that! I wanted excitement.

I needed a D-boy, a thug....a nigga who would fuck me hard while choking me and calling me a nasty bitch. Not all that I love you, slow grinding shit Mike did. That's why I couldn't help but be attracted to his best friend Dee from the jump. Dee was everything Mike wasn't, the total opposite. Almost everything about him was still the same as it was the day Mike introduced us at Carver High and we dipped off to fuck in the stairwell.

Dee was still that 5'9" and 187 lb. a light skinned street nigga with a mouth full of gold and tattoos. That freaky ass dope boy with the magic touch. Unlike Mike, Dee didn't turn soft and want to live some fairytale ass life he'd never have. No, Dee was everything I liked with no strings attached. At least I thought there was no strings attached, but I was beginning to see that nigga was falling in love too. I didn't need all that shit though. All I wanted was the dick whenever I needed it. I didn't need another Mike always up under me and trying to control everything.

"Helllllll, NO!" I said out loud to myself as I tried to shake the thoughts running through my head.

After drying off and rubbing lotion all over my body, I went into my bedroom to put on my black laced thong panties when my cell began to ring. I looked at the screen and saw that it was Dee calling. I felt my heart start to race and my pussy start to get wet because I knew his call meant that he was close by or on his way; either way, he was coming to give me what I wanted and needed the most, and I was ready for it. After putting on my black silk robe and spraying some Dolce and Gabbana perfume, I grabbed my cell off the dresser and stopped to look at myself in the mirror before I answered it.

I looked so sexy and seductive in my black lace with my robe flowing open. However, my eyes still revealed the hurt and emptiness inside I always tried to hide from the world. I could see passed my rough, tough exterior right to the dysfunctional, hurt little girl inside of me. I hated seeing her because she was weak. She couldn't take care of herself and makes sure no one hurt her and I resented her for that. I liked the person I had become more. I liked the man-eater that I was. I had to smirk at myself as I shook off the remorseful feelings I sometimes felt. I was exactly who I needed to be in order to get what I wanted.

"Hello." I said into the phone while still admiring all of my sexiness in the mirror.

My voice cracked a little as I spoke, taking me off guard as I tried to be my normal, dominating self. I had to remain in control, yet that vulnerable little girl inside of me didn't know when to get lost. She was the one who made me relive the past and face my feelings. Sometimes I could ignore her and other times I couldn't; but regardless of the outcome, she always made me face realities about myself I would rather stay blind to. She was the reason for my constant internal fight; always trying to get me to analyze situations and thinking logically.

The problem was I didn't want to think logically nor did I want to care about what other people thought of me. However, I sometimes did and that shit drove me crazy. I was tired of people always judging me and assuming I was a certain way. That's why I gave them exactly what they wanted. If they wanted to say I was a hoe, then I'd show them a hoe. The best he they'd ever seen. I found out from a therapist when I was seventeen that I acted out because I thought that's what people expected of me. She said that I knew right from wrong, but chose wrong because it was easier and more convenient. She was right just like my aunt was right when she would tell me I was rotten.

When I was nine, she told me that I was just like a red apple. She said that I was all shiny and beautiful on the outside, tempting people to bite me and taste my juicy center. However, she said when you finally did take that bite, you found out that it was all a facade. That seemingly beautiful, potentially delicious apple was all a fantasy. Inside of that beautiful creation was nothing it appeared to be. The inside was hollow...empty, void of life. She was right. All I desired was fulfilling the urges of my flesh, satisfying that deep yearning. Dee gave me what I yearned for.

"Wasup baby. Is daddy's pussy wet and ready yet?" Dee asked me and then sucked his teeth.

Ummm, his fine ass made me wet just thinking about him. I couldn't help but blush as I sat down on the bed. He made me forget everything that little girl inside of me tried to dig up. My lust for him drowned out all of the sadness whenever I heard his voice. He was my refuge.

"Yes daddy. Kitty Kat is ready to be petted so she can purrrr." I say seductively as I ran my fingers across my thick, smooth thighs and up to my pussy.

All I wanted to do at that moment was feel Dee's arms around me and his big dick inside of me, helping to quench that growing thirst inside. I yearned for a man's touch, his love, and his affection. I guess growing up with no mama, no daddy, and being raised by a lesbian aunt who raped, beat, and tricked me out to her friends since I was six had that effect on me. Some people would say it fucked me up, but I think it just opened my eyes to the world. It taught me to look out for me whenever I could and to disregard everyone else's feelings in order to make myself happy. That's why I didn't give a fuck about being a hoe and fucking every nigga I ran across. No one ever gave a fuck about me enough to save me.

As long as I fulfilled my urges and got money to take care of my kids, nothing else mattered...not even hurting Mike. Even though he saved me and showed me love I never had, I didn't owe him shit. I didn't tell him to beat the man he caught raping me in my aunt's living room as she watched. I didn't ask him to go crazy and beat my aunt and him within an inch of their lives before whisking me away to safety.

Although I was grateful for what Mike did for me, I didn't ask him to do it; therefore, I didn't owe him shit. I owed myself happiness that's all. Me, Alia Baldwin...no one else. Hell, half of the time I felt I didn't even owe my kids anything. I loved them with all of me, but that selfish, neglected little girl inside me never let me fully love and care for them the way I should have. I knew they had Mike and that he was a much better parent for them. He needed them and they needed him. All I needed was to fill that deep, nagging, dull feeling in my heart and stop the constant throbbing between my legs. To do that I needed dick and Dee had plenty to give.

"Ummmm daddy, I'm waiting." I whispered into the phone to Dee seductively as I continued to run my fingers up and down my body.

I felt an intense desire and lust take over me as I panted into the phone and ran my fingers across my pussy.

"Bet that. Daddy will be there in 15 minutes. You be ready because I'm gonna give you this KING DICK when I get there. I know yo junky ass been feignin.'" Dee said laughing.

I almost cursed him the fuck out, but I had to face the fact that he was telling the truth. I was a nympho through and though...always had been and probably always would be. With an aunt who started making me touch and lick on her at six and passed me out to her friends like gum, what else could I have been? From the age of six to fifteen, I existed strictly for my aunt and her friend's sick sexual pleasures. I had done nastier, downright disgusting shit by the age of ten than some people would ever do in their lifetime. I lost everything living with my aunt; my innocence, my sense of hope, and my desire to live a so-called normal life.

By the time I met Mike one day when I was stealing food out of the grocery store he worked in, I had almost given up on everything good in life. After he caught me eating bologna out of the pack and sticking bread and bottled waters down my pant legs, I was willing to give my body to him in exchange for him not snitching. I guess my blatant hoe-ness took him by surprise because he quickly gave me the food and tried to discourage me from giving myself away so easily. I saw a caring and compassionate look in Mike's eyes that day I had never saw from anyone, and it scared the shit out of me.

I never remembered the love and attention I must have gotten from my parents before they died in a car accident when I was five. All I knew was pain, anger, and sex which were all of the things my aunt had taught me. I resisted the love Mike offered and decided to use his love to manipulate him for my own benefit. By then the damage of my abusive, emotionally and psychologically crippling, dysfunctional upbringing was already done and there was no turning back. Sex had me hooked so I sunk my claws into Mike and continued to fuck any and every nigga I wanted to, making sure I got paid at the same time.

That all changed though as I got closer to Mike for a while anyway. For about three months I fought my urges, silencing my screams as I remained faithful to only him. That shit quickly ended the first day he introduced me to Dee. Dee and I fucked in the stairwell at school as Mike sat in class, and after I got my much needed nut that nigga gave me $100 of his weed money. That's the moment I had a hoe-phiany. I knew that I had a jewel between my legs niggas would pay for, and I had to start charging their asses. If they wanted some of my juicy berry, they had to be ready to pay the fee, simple as that.

That's what I lived by, but Dee was a little different though. He knew exactly how to fuck me. He was the only man who could make me cum, but that was the only thing I wanted from him. No, I needed it so badly I could feel it inside of me.

"Oohhhh daddy, you know I'm feignin'. I need you....I want to deep throat that dick and drink every last drop of your juices over and over again. Ummm!" I moaned as I slid my lace panties to the side and began to massage my clit slowly.

I could hear Dee breathing hard as hell on the other end and horns blast in the background as he made his way to me. I almost laughed out loud at his anxiousness, but that urge inside of me pulled me deeper and deeper into a lust filled haze. I needed him just as much as he wanted me, but I was also enjoying the power I had over him. I guess that was the power of the pussy my aunt always preached about. I figured it had to have some truth in it because I put a hold on every nigga I touched. I could string them along and get them to do my bidding with little effort, while all along all I really wanted and needed was the dick. That's the only thing that dulled the pain.

I continued to massage my clit and moan into the phone, spinning my web around Dee.

"Ohhhh daddy hurry. I need you. My pussy is so wet right now. I want you inside of me...I need you inside of me. I want to feel that big dick throb inside of me as you choke me into the organism of my life. I need that daddy. Can you give that to me?" I asked Dee panting as I fingered myself hard and fast.

I could hear Dee gasp and then laugh as he revved his car's engine, pushing it faster and closer to me.

"Dammmmnnn, forreal bae... that's how you doing it? SHIIDDD, I'm fina fly to that muthafucka!" Dee said as I heard his car's engine revv again and he blew his horn. "Move muthafucka, DAMNN!" Dee yelled frantically at other motorists as I succumbed to my urge to laugh.

I almost lost my groove laughing at Dee as I imagined him driving like a bat out of hell to get to me. Juicy had that nigga crazy and I was enjoying every minute.

"Don't kill yourself daddy. Ms. Kitty will be here waiting...dripping wet for that big, pink dick. Umm..." I said as I continued to finger myself, fast and hard.

Suddenly, I felt it rising up from the depths of my pussy, into my stomach, and then up into my chest.....That Orgasm that I so desperately chased, that highest high...my CRACK!

"Agghhh, bye daddy. I'm about...to ...cummmm!" I said as the floodgates broke and my orgasm rushed over me in strong, forceful waves.

I hung up the phone as my body began to shake violently. I laid on my back still moving my cum covered fingers in and out of my pussy until every burst of energy inside of me was gone.

"DAMNNN!" I said out loud to myself as the euphoria like feeling from the orgasm subsided and the room came back into focus.

"I fuck myself better than any nigga." I said out loud to myself laughing as I got up off of the bed.

I knew that I could get that crack I needed by myself, but I needed a nigga too. "Ain't nothing like some good dick attached to big money." I said to myself as I headed to the bathroom to take a quick shower before Dee arrived.

Chapter 3

<u>Dee</u>

I pushed my new 2013 Dodge Charger to 85 mph, weaving in and out of traffic trying to make it to LiLi. I hated to admit it to myself, but I was feeling her thick ass. Damn, that bitch….that bitch made a nigga feel like a kid again. Too bad she wasn't mine, not yet anyway. I was going to get her though, I had to. Hell, I saw her first anyway. I was outside on the block getting my money when I saw her fine ass rush into the grocery store. I came in a few minutes later to cuff her fine ass, but I saw Mike talking to her instead. He was like my brother so I bowed out and let him have her. I didn't know that his sensitive ass was gonna wife the bitch knowing she fucked any and everybody.

I knew plenty old heads in the hood who said they had fucked her and the young niggas were just as eager to tell their stories about Lick Em' Low LiLi. She was the hoe of the hood and everybody but Mike knew it. I was gonna change that though. Mike had fucked up from the start trying to save her. A bitch like her didn't want to be saved by a weak ass nigga. He couldn't get her to settle down, trying to love on her and be all soft. I knew just what the bitch needed to get some act right. A good ass whooping and regular doses of super good dick would have her hoeish ass acting right real quick, and that's what I would give her. It was fuck Mike's feelings when it came to that situation. That 'bros before hoes' bullshit was out the window. LiLi was my bitch, not his.

Yo Gotti's song, *Sorry,* blasted through my speakers, shaking the windows of every car I passed and putting me in straight beast mode.

"I can't fuck wit you no mo hoe and I'm sorry. You a disloyal ass bitch, hoe you sorry. You probably ain't pregnant...hoe, you flauging. That probably ain't my baby, I need Maury." I yelled out of the window, rapping the lyrics to the song with Gotti as I inhaled the Kush blunt I had just lit.

Damn that nigga was always saying some real shit. It was like he wrote that song for LiLi's sneaky, hoeish, fine ass. Her sexy, deceitful ass swore up and down Alaya was my daughter and not Mike's, but I couldn't see that being true, knowing she fucked everybody.

"Gotti probably fucked her too as much as she was in the Crest back in the day..... Damn this hoe in my head." I said to myself as I hit the slab heading from North Memphis to the Haven and straight to LiLi.

Despite how much I resented her hoeish ways, I couldn't deny the fact that LiLi had a hold on me. I didn't want to have feelings for her or to even see her as anything but a great fuck. However, shit happened. Feelings somehow got involved and I found myself looking forward to seeing her more and more. I just couldn't let that bitch get in my mind like she had Mike's crazy ass. That nigga had woke me up at 7 a.m. that morning as he was on his way to work, talking about some white muthafucka named Stuart who sent LiLi a dick picture. My guy was the hardest nigga in the hood, stay talking shit, but he was weak as a muthafucka when it came to that bitch! She had that maine's head all the way fucked up.

That's why he should have let me have her. He couldn't control her from the jump, but I could. He was all sniffling and shit, crying about what he did for her while I was sitting there deciding what position I was gona try on the bitch later on. That was the game....he knew what it was, or at least he used to. That was our game most of our lives, any bitch was prey. That was until him and LiLi got married in 2012. After that from birth to the dirt, straight gangsta homeboy turned into a lil' bitch.

I didn't even know what to say to him when he told me that he loved the bitch more than he loved himself. All I could think was, what the fuck? I knew that I would never love anybody that damn much, especially not no going ass bitch. However, LiLi was bad as hell. That bitch did things with her mouth that made a nigga want to curl up in the fetal position and suck his fucking thumb. She was a real nigga's downfall all wrapped up in a sexy, seductive package. That bitch had me fucked up though.

I wanted LiLi and all, but she wasn't gonna play me like she did them other niggas. She wasn't gonna have me crying and sniffling and shit, wanting to kill her ass. Hell no, I'd never get that bad. I'd walk the fuck away from that bitch, her fye cap, and that big, juicy pussy before I'd let her turn me into a bitch. I just had to stay on my shit whenever I was around her. I knew that bitch was so up on game from being out in the streets. She probably thought she had me sprung.

She had me fucked up, thinking I was one of them lame as niggas she tricked out of money. I gave to the bitch because I wanted too, not in an effort to pay her so-called fee. I knew about every nigga she tricked off with; even though deep down I wanted to wife her someday, she had to get her shit all the way together first. As a matter-of-fact, I had to get my shit together too because I was enjoying the bachelor's life getting money and getting good pussy from whomever I wanted when I wanted it.

LiLi had that bomb ass pussy too. She had that suction shit, all gripping and squishy. The type of pussy that sucked a nigga's soul right out of his body, and she was a straight money maker on top of that. That's why I had decided long ago to play my cards right and keep that hoe close. I gave her those much needed doses of good dick and a little cash in hopes of reaping some of her tricking cash in return. I would gain her trust then flip it on the bitch and pimp her while keeping my ongoing pussy appointments.

"Yea, that'll work." I said to myself smiling as I got lost in my thoughts.

I'd ride that shit until the wheels fell off as long as Mike's crazy ass didn't find out. *'That maniac can't ever find out about this.'* I thought to myself as I pulled into his and LiLi's driveway.

I turned off the ignition and hurriedly got out of my car, hitting the alarm as I walked up on to the porch and straight into the house. LiLi always left the door unlocked for me and if she wasn't waiting for me at the front door, I knew to take my ass to the bedroom for my surprise. As soon as I walked into the bedroom and smelled the aroma from LiLi's perfume, my dick got hard.

"Hey boo." LiLi's fine ass said to me coming out of the bathroom in nothing but a pink thong and some six-inch diamond studded stilettos.

"Damn," was all I could say as I began to quickly take my clothes off. I kept my eyes glued on LiLi as I quickly removed my clothing and she stood there with her finger in her mouth, rubbing her pussy and teasing me.

"Aye, come here sexy!" I yelled as I stood up naked, stroking my dick and licking my lips.

LiLi shook her head no and stepped backwards into the bathroom, testing me and agitating that animal in me. I wanted her sexy, soft ass in front of me right then and I wasn't ready to take no for an answer. I stepped up towards LiLi as she extended her arm, telling me to stop.

"I only come to my daddy, and my daddy wouldn't say no bitch shit like that. My daddy knows what to say to get this pussy wet." LiLi said taunting me again while licking her own nipples.

That bitch wanted to play. She loved for a nigga to dominate her. She always wanted me to curse her out when we fucked...choke her and fuck her hard. I didn't know what the fuck had happened to her in her past, but I knew that somebody had fucked her up and turned her out. *'Lucky for me.'* I thought as I switched back into beast mode just like she liked it.

"Get yo funky ass over here bitch." I yelled taking the belt out of my pants and laying it across the bed.

I could see LiLi's eyes light up from across the room at the sight of my belt as she quickly ran and stood in front of me, staring at me with a seductive look. Her nipples were hard as she stood there and her breasts heaved. She had this pained, yet passionate look on her face as she pleaded for the dick with her eyes. That bitch was a real fucking freak and I was just the nigga for her.

"On yo knees bitch!" I yelled at LiLi as I stepped to the side and slapped her on the left ass cheek with my dick.

She looked at me with a longing in her eyes that made my dick grow harder. I was starting to feel a yearning to be inside of her soft, wet center, but I tried to fight it and stay in control.

"What have I told you about playing with a G, bitch? Now open yo damn mouth and suck this dick." I yelled at LiLi as she opened her mouth to say something and I shoved my dick as far down her throat as I could.

I had to smirk as she took all of my dick into her mouth with no problem while moaning and looking up at me, enticing me with her eyes. Unlike basic bitches, LiLi was a pro and just like All-State. Whenever I was with her, my dick was always in good hands. She took care of me by always giving me what I wanted and I satisfied her by giving her what she needed.

I quickly put my right hand around LiLi's throat and applied a little pressure as she slobbed up and down my dick. Both of us moaned softly, enjoying the moment of peaceful pleasure. I tried not to show my emotions when dealing with bitches, but LiLi was different. I couldn't hide the way I truly felt when I was with her. Moans and shit just slipped out whenever I was caught up in the moment.

LiLi's mouth felt so good I could feel my manhood growing inside of her jaw. For a second I started to panic because I could also feel the nut rushing up through my balls, sending sensations throughout my body. I couldn't let her get off that easy though. I had to take control of the situation and punish LiLi's pussy like she needed me to do. I took my dick out of her mouth and slapped it across her right cheek as I grabbed a fist full of her hair.

"Bitch you want this dick?" I asked her as I rubbed the head of my dick all over her face, leaving pre-cum trails on her eyelids, chin, and brows.

The thought must have excited her freaky ass to her peak because suddenly she started moaning loudly as she stuck her fingers deep into her big, juicy pussy.

"Ohhh yes I want it...I need it daddy." LiLi whined through her moans, exciting me even more.

At that moment that bitch had me feignin' just like her. Like a sex fiend looking for another hit, I was open and only LiLi could give me exactly what I needed.

"Beg for it then if you need it so badly." I yelled at LiLi taunting her like she did me as I stroked my dick in her face.

I watched her body tense up and a glossy look form in her eyes as she begged me to give her the drug she so desperately needed.

"Pleassseee give it to me daddy. Dee please give me that dick." She begged as I shoved my dick back into her mouth and proceeded to fuck her face.

I knew that was exactly what she wanted because as soon as I did that her hands were on my ass cheeks as she devoured my dick, pulling me deeper and deeper in her mouth and down her throat. LiLi was a real fucking pro...a true dick magician.

I closed my eyes and held my head back as she did a flicking motion on my dick head. The pleasure LiLi was lavishing on me had my mind so cloudy I almost forgot I had beef with her ass. Just then I remembered that Mike had told me she sucked his dick after he found the picture in her phone. I knew that was her way of pacifying him. I wasn't about to let her get away with that...oh yea, I was slick jealous and for that I owed that bitch one.

I let LiLi continue her pleasure mission for a couple more minutes before I took my dick out of her mouth again, slapping her even harder across the face with it. It was time for me to give that bitch the pleasure mixed with pain she craved while satisfying my own need for revenge. I know jealousy seemed stupid being that technically she was with my best friend. However, we had an unspoken code, LiLi and I. She knew that she wasn't supposed to be giving no nigga my mouth. That was supposed to belong to me and me only. She would have to pay for that.

"Aw yea...I heard you been giving my mouth away. You been giving my shit away LiLi? You sucked Mike's dick this morning?" I asked stepping back away from her as she still kneeled on the floor.

I grabbed my belt off the bed as I began to walk around LiLi slowly.

"You been a bad bitch, huh?" I asked LiLi as I watched her eyes glow at the thought of me beating her with my belt.

My bitch was extra freaky, but I liked it. I grabbed her in the back of her hair and made her stand to her feet as I stared into her eyes. In her eyes I could see excitement, her need to be dominated, and a little hint of fear. I knew that she was totally enjoying the freaky, sick sex game we were playing. I was giving her the fantasy, hard fucking she wanted...the shit Mike couldn't give her.

"Lay face down." I yelled at her as I released her hair and pushed her on to the bed.

LiLi quickly obeyed my commands and got on the bed face down, tooting her ass up in the air and right in my face. I ripped the pink thong from her body as I stared at her big, round, caramel ass.

It was so smooth and luscious, I couldn't help but to bite it.

"Ummm yes daddy...I been a bad girl. Punish me." LiLi moaned as I stepped back away from the bed while wrapping my belt around my hand and admiring the bite mark I left on her ass cheek.

LiLi looked back at me and winked as I slapped her ass cheek and thought about how she was kinky as fuck. She had let me do anything I wanted to do to her up until that point, so I had to see exactly how far I could go. I bet she would let me beat her within an inch of death if that meant the best orgasm of her life. I decided to test that theory by slicing her as hard as I could across the back with my belt.

I gave her ass a slave whack, leaving a huge welt on her velvety skin as she moaned in pleasure.

She looked back at me again with a high, glossy look in her eyes as I thought the pulsating in my dick would drive me crazy. I stroked my rock hard manhood fast and hard before grabbing a condom off the nightstand and quickly slipping it on. I knew LiLi hated condoms, but she had me fucked up. She was fucking way too many niggas for me to take the chance of getting her pregnant.

I always wore a condom when I fucked her. I only had one break on me once with her, that's why she said Alaya was mine. I knew she didn't have anything because I was with her for her monthly check-ups. It was that baby shit I wanted no parts of. Besides, I still didn't trust that I know who her baby daddy is, shit, and I couldn't trust her so I made sure the condom was on properly before slicing her on the ass with my belt again.

I watched as welts quickly began to appear on her back and ass cheeks as I continued to hit her and she moaned like she was in heaven. I wanted to stop when I saw blood drip from one of the spots I struck on her leg, but she kept moaning and begging me to continue. I struck her once more on the ass, giving her the pain she wanted before I stuck my dick in her hard and deep, causing her whole body to tense up. I struck her across the left cheek hard with the belt as I dug deeper inside of her wet love box, and felt her body start to relax.

I kept slicing LiLi on the ass and back with my belt as I thrust my dick deeper and deeper in her trying to touch that g-spot. The more I hit LiLi the more she moaned, and the more she moaned the harder my dick got, causing me to drill her into the mattress. After about 10 minutes of that, we were both covered in sweat and making noises I had never made before. I didn't know what the fuck it was, but LiLi had a way of flipping a situation and dominating a nigga with her pussy even though she wanted him to be in control.

As I was hitting her from the back while pulling her long, black hair, and enjoying the way her fat ass bounced back against my pelvis, she turned to look at me and told me to choke her with the belt.

"Tie it around my neck daddy like I'm a dog and fuck me. I'm yo bitch daddy...now do me." LiLi said taunting me again, pushing me to fulfill her perverse sexual desires.

I couldn't believe my luck of finding a bitch so freaky and uninhibited as I looped the belt around her neck like a noose and fucked her like it was the end of the world. LiLi fucked me back, grinding her hips and making her fat ass smack against my stomach with force, creating a loud smacking sound. I shivered and held on to her like I was riding a runaway stallion as she bucked and fucked me, squeezing her pussy walls. That is when I realized she had tricked me again. She was fucking me. I suddenly began to feel her body shudder beneath me as she bit the sheets and yelled out my name.

"DEEEEEEE...yessssss. I'm coming baby...." LiLi yelled as her orgasm came in hard and fast like waves in the ocean.

I could feel my nut on the brink of eruption too as I held on to LiLi's bucking body until her spasms of euphoria subsided. After bouncing her ass a few more times, LiLi slipped from under me and sat up in the bed, snatching the rubber off my dick and putting it all in her mouth. She sucked me hard and fast until I came all down her throat. I could feel my knees shaking as she drunk all of me and massaged my balls, while looking into my eyes. At that moment, I knew that all of my resistance was for nothing. I knew right then that LiLi had me too and I would never be the same again.

Part 2

Secrets Revealed: The Creation of a Beast

Chapter 4

<u>Mike</u>

The two days following me finding a dick picture in LiLi's phone were hell. I had to fight the urge to smack the shit out of her whenever she was around, which wasn't often. Even though she had gotten caught up and knew I was still kind of salty about the whole situation, she was still running the streets and ignoring her responsibilities as a mother and wife. I was doing more and more at home and seeing less and less of her. It was like all I did was wake up, go to work, pick up the kids, fix dinner, and clean the house, and then go to bed to start my mundane day all over again.

When LiLi was at home all she did was sit on her ass with that fucking phone in her hand, yelling at the kids to be quiet. She never tried to connect with them or show them the love and attention a mother would. She cared more about herself than anything else and that's the part of LiLi I hated. Still, I couldn't bring myself to leave her because I loved her so much. I took the neglect and sometimes verbal abuse from LiLi, holding it inside and letting it begin a slow boiling anger in my heart.

I silenced the evil voices in my head telling me what LiLi was doing and turned those ugly feelings into love I could use to nurture my kids enough for two people. I was like a fucking super dad. I washed, cooked, cleaned, read to the kids, did hair, and took them to church every opportunity I could. I loved them even more than I loved LiLi and I knew that even if I lost her, I would always have them no matter what.

I needed them and they needed me. Aside from the magnetic, unexplainable hold LiLi had on me linked to our sexual and emotional connection, it was our kids that kept me with her over the years. It was them who made me stay when shit got too much for one nigga to deal with. It was also the kids who kept me from snapping LiLi's fucking neck whenever I caught her doing sneaky shit.

I went over the events of the last few days in my mind as I got ready to leave work. It was Friday, pay day, and I knew LiLi would be at home waiting on me to give her funky ass some money for her hair, nails, and any other materialistic bullshit her heart desired. LiLi was greedy and money hungry like that. She had her own job and money, but she wanted mine too. She always complained that the money I brought in as the Building and Operations Manager at the Agricenter wasn't enough, but her bug eyed ass had her hand out every Friday, it never failed.

I left work in a numb trance just thinking about all of the lies and pain LiLi had put me through. I buried all of those feelings deep inside once I stopped at my mother's house and picked up the kids. The way that they ran to me and jumped in my arms made me momentarily forget about the anger and resentment that was building up inside of me for their mother. All I could feel was their love and how they were excited to see their daddy. After stopping at McDonald's to get five Happy Meals like I did for the kids every Friday, I headed home with the intentions of letting everything go for the moment and focusing on keeping my kids happy and in the home with two parents.

When I got into the house, it was just as I thought. LiLi was waiting for me. She sat in my recliner with her black sweat pants, *Fuck you, Pay Me* tank top, and flip flops on, rolling her eyes and chewing bubble gum as she cut the thread that attached the extensions to her head. I knew that was her before the club attire she wore to get her hair, nails, and lashes done, and I hated that shit. However, I didn't feel like arguing about that same hoe routine she did every week, so I just dropped $300 on the coffee table and walked into the kitchen to grab a beer.

I could hear LiLi's gum popping stop suddenly and her mumble to herself as I sat at the kitchen table and popped the top on my 32 oz. Bud Light. I took a big gulp and enjoyed the tingly feeling in my body as it slid down my throat while watching LiLi come into the kitchen from the corner of my eye. She stood there with her hand on her hip rolling her eyes with her lips turned up as if she smelled something funky.

I know my initial reaction must have thrown her off because she expected me to act a fool like I did every Friday. She was waiting on me to preach about family and her being a mother and wife who stays home. However, I didn't do what she expected that time. I was tired of doing that and fighting to keep her home when I knew she didn't give a fuck. It was like my mama always said, "Nothing can keep a person who doesn't want to be kept. The more you try; the more you lose yourself."

I was tired of losing myself and I was prepared to let LiLi go for a while until she valued me and all that I did. I guess LiLi felt I was done because before I knew it her ratchet, I-don't-give-a-fuck demeanor was replaced by the meek, docile

LiLi I only saw when she wanted something. It was clear she wasn't ready to lose me and all of the benefits having me around offered. However, she knew that I would never satisfy her the way she wanted me to and she would never be able to give me the happy, monogamous woman I needed and wanted. She didn't give a fuck though...she just wanted what she needed.

"Mike baby, what's wrong with you. I ain't never seen you come home on a Friday and just drop off money that easily. What's up? You in yo feelings and shit, huh?" LiLi said sighing as I calmly sipped my beer while staring straight ahead.

I had no intentions of answering her smart ass at that moment because if I did I would probably have to choke the fuck out of her after calling her every bitch in the book. Instead of going off, I just turned to look at her and smiled before replying with a blank expression on my face.

"Naw LiLi, I ain't in my feelings and shit. Do you, boo. Go get yo muthafucking hair done, nails done, and get them long ass spider lashes put on your face. After getting all Hoed Up go yo thirsty ass on to the club with yo hoeish ass friend. Ignore your family like you always do. It's yo world LiLi, live it up." I told the bitch as I held the anger brewing inside.

I wanted to smack that little smug ass smile off her face as she rolled her eyes at me and popped her lips.

"I knew you was tripping about that. That's why I told Tasha to come over here to do my hair and stuff. Now you can't say I'm running off and shit. I even ordered some pizzas and got some movies for us to watch before I go out later. If that's okay with you big daddy even though you mad at yo bookie." LiLi said scooting next to me and poking her bottom lip out to pout like she always did when she fucked up.

I wanted to flip her ass out of the chair and walk away, but the love I had for her won me over like it always did. Before I knew it, I smiled at her and she used that as an opportunity to reel me in. LiLi kissed me gently on the neck and rubbed her double d titties on my arm as I deeply inhaled her scent. I loved her little lying ass and like always, she had me right where she wanted me. I was under her spell as she kissed all over me and told me how much she loved me.

I left the kitchen to take my shower with a big ass grin on my face. It was like LiLi's touch was magical. She made me momentarily forget about everything just from her touch. I felt as if I were floating as I got undressed in our master bathroom, turned on the water, and prepared to take a hot shower. Just as I was about to get into the shower, I stepped on something hard and had to look down to see what it was. There on the floor lie the tip of a black-n-mild. Before I could even process what was now in my hand, I could feel rage and worry rush over me. Somebody had been in my fucking house, in my bathroom to be exact, smoking a black-n-mild. Being that neither I nor LiLi smoked any form of tobacco other than the cigars we rolled blunts in, I knew the tip of the black-n-mild had to belong to some nigga.

I turned off the shower and sat on the toilet with the black-n-mild tip in my hand as my mind reeled from anger and the thick heat fog in the bathroom. I couldn't believe that LiLi had just won me over, professing her love for me and only me, knowing that some nigga was just in my house. Tears ran from my eyes as I squeezed the piece of plastic between my fingers. I wanted to go down stairs and fuck LiLi up for ruining my happiness again. However, I knew my kids were home and I never wanted them to see me angry, let alone violent with their mommy. I had to be smart and think of some way to hurt her.

The perfect plan dawned on me as I turned the shower back on, got into the shower, and washed away all of the hurt and anger I felt inside. When I stepped out of the shower, I quickly grabbed my cellphone and called my best friend Dee.

"Aye bruh, fuck what I said about kicking it with LiLi before she goes out. Fuck that hoe. Let's go hoop. I'll be over there to scoop you in about 10 minutes." I said to Dee after he answered the phone.

"Aite bruh...but what happened? You and LiLi broke up or some shit?" Dee asked me kind of catching me off guard.

I was wondering why it mattered to him what happened between me and LiLi. I knew I had told him a lot shit about our relationship over the years, but he never seemed interested. He just usually gave me his little advice and changed the subject, but now his ass was asking questions and shit. I wasn't telling him shit. Mama always told me to keep folks out of my business to keep down shit and I intended on doing that from then on.

"Oh we straight bruh. I just need to get back on the court for a minute. Show yo old ass why you need to stay in an office behind a desk." I said laughing as Dee told me to fuck myself and then we both hung up.

I felt a little better as I got dressed and went downstairs to leave. My more relaxed feeling was ruined when I walked into the living room to see LiLi's ratchet ass friend Tasha had arrived with her two bad ass kids. My living room was a disaster

79

with weave tracks, bobby pins, glue, finger nail polish, lashes, and children everywhere. I wanted to shake the fuck out of LiLi and Tasha for being so damn trifling, but I knew it was useless. Tasha rolled her eyes at me as I walked into the room and kissed each one of my kids on their foreheads. I sucked my teeth at her as I walked back passed her out of the room. Suddenly, I could hear Tasha ask LiLi where her temporary man was going, and that's when the cursing began.

"Uhh excuse me Mike, but where the fuck are you going? You complain I'm never here; but when I organize a movie night, you think yo WEAK ASS fina go. Oh hell no you not." LiLi said smacking her lips as she got up out of the dining room chair they had sitting in the middle of my living room floor.

Looking at her standing there with half of her head braided and the other half filled with 30 inch tracks made me laugh as I turned back to face her. Now who was in their feelings? It felt good having the upper hand for a second, so I had to bask in the moment by just standing there and smiling at LiLi for a while. I watched as she got irritated and wondered where I was running off to in such a hurry. That bitch was so blind with jealousy for the first time she didn't even notice I had on basketball shorts and a white t, which made it obvious I was about to go hoop.

"Wouldn't you like to know Yamp ass LiLi. Don't worry about me. I'm temporary remember?? Just like yo Big Bird looking ass friend over there just said. You shouldn't worry about temporary people because you're the last thing on my mind." I said before turning and walking out of the door, leaving that maggot standing there with her mouth open.

I laughed all the way to Dee's house and to the court thinking about the look on LiLi's face when I called her a yamp and told her I wasn't thinking about her. I could barely concentrate on the game at first as visions of LiLi at home mad as fuck, continuously flashed in my mind. I bet she was imagining me fucking a bitch at the very moment I was blocking all of Dee's weak ass shots. With every thought of LiLi at home suffering as I had, my shots got better and better.

I guess my sudden control over my love life was giving me extra energy because I was a beast out there on the court. Everything I threw up, I hit and I was all over every nigga I d'ed up. I was out there getting my Lebron on forreal, so much so I had nigga's on Dee team mad as hell. By the end of the second game, a big, tall, light skinned nigga named Rozel was so hot he felt he had to say something to me. That was the worst mistake that bitch ass nigga could have made.

"Damn, niggas out here playing like they in the NBA or some shit. If a muthafucka was a true MVP, he'd be able to keep his hoe at home. Yet every nigga in the hood done had a piece of Lick Em' Low LiLi, the Mrs. Wayans of the hood with all them damn kids. Even ME....but I ain't the pappy!" Rozel said laughing as I ran back down the court to make a layup.

All I could hear was the laughter from all of the other niggas on the court and Dee yelling for me not to do it as I ran back towards Rozel. When I got back to him standing there laughing like he was on Comic View, you would have thought I was a football player rather than basketball player. I grabbed Rozel's legs and slammed him back on to the cement so fast he didn't even know what hit his ass. Before he could blink, think, or react, I was on top of him dropping fists and forearm strikes into his face and head. Rage took over me, igniting an anger that consumed every part of me. I hit him over and over, unleashing every negative feeling I had been holding over the past few days. Nothing and no one around me existed at that moment. All I wanted to do was kill that nigga.

The next thing I knew Dee and a couple more of my homies were pulling me off a bloody, unconscious Rozel.

"Mike, stop maine...come on." Dee said as he pushed me towards my truck.

I was frozen for a second as I stared at Rozel's bloody, battered face, wondering had the pussy learned his lesson. I wouldn't let him or any other nigga disrespect me or LiLi in my face. Yeah, she was a nasty little slut, but she was MY nasty little slut and I was the only muthafucka who had the right to say it. He didn't have that right and he never had the right to bring my kids in shit. I bet his pussy ass learned that.

I jumped into my Expedition and balled out of the park's parking lot going 100 mph as I raged about LiLi and what Rozel had said. I could see the fear and anxiety in Dee's eyes as I weaved in and out of traffic, pushing my truck faster and faster.

"I can't believe this bitch keep doing this shit to me. I'm going to kill this bitch and any nigga she fucking. She got me fucked up. She can't do this shit to me after all I did for her." I yelled through my tears as I hit the steering wheel with my fist and continued to drive erratically.

LiLi had my mind so gone at that moment, I couldn't concentrate on shit, not even driving safely. I needed to hear her voice. I needed to hear her explanation at that moment. I needed to hear her tell me everything was a lie and it would be alright, even if it wasn't the truth. I quickly found my phone in my pocket and pushed the button to speed dial LiLi's cell phone.

My heart raced and I felt as if my head would explode as I waited for LiLi to answer. I had so many questions and scenarios running through my mind I felt like I was going insane and I couldn't rest until that bitch told me something. I waited and cursed as I drove toward Dee's house with the phone still ringing in my hand.

"I don't wonna kill this bitch, but I think I will if she fucks me over." I said to Dee as I pushed my truck to 80 mph, weaving through traffic.

Chapter 5

LiLi

"Bzzz…..Bzzz…..Bzzz." My cell phone went off, scaring the fuck out of me and irritating me at the same damn time.

I stopped what I was doing to look at the caller ID and see that it was Mike calling.

"What the fuck does he want?" I asked myself out loud before answering the phone and hearing Mike yell hysterically on the other end.

"LiLi, what the fuck? Maine, bitch I'ma kill you. What the fuck you out here doing in the hood? I got niggas confronting me on the muthafucking basketball court, talking about you Lick Em' Low LiLi in the hood and you fucking everybody. What the FUCK LiLi? Tell me something. How the fuck do you know that nigga Rozel? Get to muthafucking talking ALIA!!" Mike yelled in my ear like a fucking madman.

I knew that nigga was serious from the hostility in his voice, so I quickly stood up and walked out of the room to gain control of the conversation. I hadn't heard him that heated in a while, but I was seeing that rage more often since my shenanigans had start being exposed. I took a deep breath as I held the phone and searched my mind for the perfect lie. I could hear Mike driving like a fool, cursing, and sniffling through the phone as I thought.

I couldn't believe that nigga was crying. He was nothing like the Mike I had fallen in love with. That was part of the reason I treated him the way that I did...he let me. I wanted him to assert himself and show me who the fuck was the boss. However, all he did was nag and moan like a bitch.

Where was the Mike of the past who would tell me to shut the fuck up at random? I missed him, but I still needed the shell of a man he had become so I put on my best wifey voice.

"Baby, calm down please. Mike you know how the niggas in our hood are...we've been here before. All they broke asses want what you got so what's the best way to get it...Hating of course. Remember when the nigga down the street texted you and said he was fucking me in his car when me and you was laying in the bed when the text came through? That's how them bitch ass niggas do because they know you got a good woman and you're happy. They don't wonna see us happy baby...don't let them steal our happiness." I said to Mike as I sniffled and pretended to cry.

I smirked to myself as I heard him sniffle and his tone soften as his tough shell began to crack.

"Baby don't cry. I'm just saying though LiLi...why this shit always happening? Why niggas always talking about they been with you or you're theirs?" Mike asked me as I rolled my eyes and looked up at the ceiling.

I was trying to remember the feelings I used to get when I heard his voice or felt his strong arms around me. I was trying to remember that electricity that drew me to him, but it was long gone. Now I didn't feel anything when he touched me and his voice was just a big, whiny ball of noise. I still loved him because of our history and my small inkling of hope that things would be like the past again. However, I think I had fallen out of love with him the day he came home from jail. Yet, I still couldn't let him go...call me selfish, but I couldn't let another bitch get him.

"Mike baby listen. That Rozel nigga ain't shit but a hating ass nigga who lies on his dick. I promise I have never touched his garbage ass. He still mad about the day I told you when he tried to talk to me at the gas station and I shut him down. You notice whenever we see him in the hood I don't even look at his broke ass...what can I do with a nigga like him when I have a man like you? Stop letting these niggas get in yo head baby and try to ruin what you got. I'm yours and only yours, so they gonna hate. Who I lay up with every night...YOU...so fuck them haters. I love you Michael Baldwin...now and forever." I said as tears ran down my cheeks.

I was so into my speech I didn't even realize I was crying until I could feel the hot tears drop on my breasts. Damn, I was good. I deserved a fucking Oscar. I could hear Mike sniffling on the other end, telling me to stop crying as I wiped away my tears.

"LiLi, maine...you so with the shit, maine. Girl, you know I love the shit out of you. I guess that's why you keep putting me through this shit, but you know what? A Good nigga only sticks around for so long. You better get some act right before I'm gone LiLi. I don't know if I can trust you, maine!" Mike yelled into the phone going from sincere and forgiving back to irate in a matter of seconds.

He was losing his fucking mind and it kind of scared me and made me feel bad at the same time. I knew he was losing his mind because of me and I really didn't want to hurt him like that. However, I had to do what I needed to do for me. I had to keep him and still be able to do my thang at the same time.

"Baby, I know shit like this makes it hard to trust me. But baby at some point you have to stop listening to everybody else and do what your heart tells you to. You know I love you and I never want to hurt you. Fuck what everyone says. Just wait until you get home baby and we will discuss this. I'll go to the club late. We just need to discuss this." I said to Mike as I walked back into the room I was in before he called.

I waited patiently as Mike took a few minutes to take deep breaths and suck his teeth before he responded.

"Bet LiLi...we do need to talk. Even though yo ass just said that you still plan on going to club tonight, I'ma overlook that. I'm about to drop Dee off at the house and I'll be right back home. We definitely gone talk..." Mike said as I stared at the phone with a worried expression knowing that he was on his way back faster than I anticipated.

I tried to keep my shit together as I swallowed down my fear and ignored the anxiety building in my heart.

"Okay baby, I'll be th-..HERE." I said, trying to rush Mike off the phone so I could finish what I was doing and rush back home.

Just as I was about to hang up, I heard Mike yell my name and I put the phone back up to my ear.

"Yes baby." I said to Mike in a sweet, but irritated voice.

"Oh, I just wanted to tell you that I love you LiLi….......and If I EVER catch you with another nigga, both of y'all asses dead." Mike said calmly before hanging up the phone.

His voice was so cold it sent chills up and down my spine, yet I still ignored the anxiety building inside of me and prepared to finish what I was doing.

I laid my cell phone on the bed and rubbed down Patrick's chest as I got back on my knees and stuck his thick dick back into my mouth. I licked up and down his shaft while keeping my eyes on his chubby, chocolate face while he moaned and rubbed my hair. Before long I could feel his manhood pulsating in my throat so he quickly took it out of my mouth and stroked it as he ordered me to turn around.

I kneeled on the bed in the doggy style position waiting on Patrick to enter me as he changed into a new condom. When he entered me from the back I could feel the relief. That deep thirst inside of me was quenched as Patrick, one of my main tricks, beat my pussy up with no mercy.

While I fucked Patrick back and moaned out in pleasure, my mind drifted back to Mike, Dee, and the turbulent situation I was creating for myself.

I wondered would shit end bad for me knowing that I was playing with lots of men's hearts and minds. I knew that could be a deadly game to play, but for some reason I just didn't give a fuck. I didn't care about the consequences when I was fulfilling my urges and getting money. I knew that lying had consequences, but I still continued to lie to every man in my life. Hell, Mike didn't even know that I had quit my job as a pharmacy tech almost 8 months ago and was stripping at Pure Passion every night.

His delusional ass thought I was some 9-to-5 straight laced bitch living from paycheck to paycheck like his sorry ass. He just didn't know I was out in the streets banking. I was making 10 times what he made in a week in one night, if he only knew. Then there was Dee, my homie lover friend, who was now catching feelings. His sex was so good and he was the type of nigga I could kick it with, but I didn't see a future with his ass either. I didn't want a future with any nigga. I was going to be what I had always been told I was all of my life, a hoe...and that was okay with me. As long as I got my money they could call me whatever they wanted to.

I closed my eyes and welcomed the euphoria my orgasm offered as Patrick pulled my hair and drilled me into ecstasy. When it was all over, I had fulfilled my desire, collected my $600, and satisfied my need to be in control as I prepared to rush back home and beat Mike there.

Chapter 6

Dee

I felt like a straight bitch riding home from the courts with Mike, holding on to the door handle and seat belt as his crazy ass sped and weaved through traffic as he cried. That shit was like a real movie as I watched this nigga's snot like a fucking baby over the hoe of the hood. I understood how a bitch with pussy that good could make a nigga stress and maybe even smack her ass from time to time, but wanting to kill the bitch was a bit too much for me. Mike's already edgy ass was like a completely different person when it came to LiLi. That nigga was like a fucking rabbit dog ready to devour anyone or anything that stood between him and LiLi. I didn't want to be that muthafucka. I was starting to rethink even speaking to LiLi's fine ass again.

I watched some of the rage leave my nigga's body as he hung up the phone with LiLi and wiped the snot from his face. I hated to see my homie from the sandbox in so much pain, but I knew that nigga brought that shit on himself. He was the muthafucka fell in love and decided to save the hoe. Now he was so caught up in love he couldn't do shit. That was some real sad shit, especially for him.

Mike was like a fucking legend in the hood known to be a muthafucking monster when necessary. After going to jail for almost beating two grown muthafuckas to death when we were teenagers, Mike gained a rep in the hood as an OG. He was the enforcer and I was the smooth, flamboyant player. We were once an awesome ass team, but all that shit slowly changed after Mike came home from doing that bid.

That's really when I lost respect for Mike as my brother because I already had a lil' feelings for LiLi, plus I knew how he really was. When he first came home, we were out in the streets fucking everything with a small waist and a banging face, leaving our mark on every dime in the city. I didn't even feel bad about fucking LiLi at all back then because he was doing his thang and so was she. After a while though, that shit changed and Mike started acting like a real phuck boy.

All he ever wanted to do was be up under LiLi. That shit cut into my time kicking it with him and my weekly routine of fucking his bitch. That's when I started resenting his lame ass...that and the fact that he controlled everything about her. That maine was so scared of losing her he had to watch her every second. That nigga was acting like a real psycho every time I turned around and that shit made me quit fucking with him like that.

Sitting there watching his ass rage worse than I'd ever seen him do before made me wonder how far that nigga would actually go. I believed him when he said he'd kill LiLi and any nigga he ever caught her with. I was not going to be that nigga. I made a mental note to make sure I was strapped with an extra clip whenever I was around Mike from that day forward. I wasn't going to take any chances with his crazy ass.

"Bruh you aite. I know this shit hard, but I keep telling you that you gotta do what's best for you. You can't keep letting a female…some pussy push you to the point of insanity. Ain't no ass worth that bruh. If she can't be real with you, just let her ass go and I'll help you find a bitch who will be true. It's some good bitches out here bruh...we just gotta find them." I said to Mike as I watched the crazy in his eyes start to disappear.

I had to wonder if that was what love was really like because if it was I wanted no parts of that bullshit. My homie had lost his balls, his dignity, and obviously his fucking mind, messing off with a bitch. A bitch who wasn't even his, not really. I didn't want to be like that. I had to remain icy when I was with LiLi. I would continue to get that good pussy and possibly some cash and then bone out. Even though a part of me wanted to love on her sexy ass, I knew she was just a hoe and that she was no good for me or any other nigga. Yet, like Mike, I just couldn't let her go.

Suddenly, Mike pulled his Expedition into the In & Out market on Chelsea and cut off the engine. I watched him as he touched the picture of LiLi and the kids hanging from a keychain on the rearview mirror. At that moment I felt bad as hell about how the bitch was deceiving him, knowing that Alaya was my daughter and not his. I wanted to tell him so bad, but I wasn't no muthafucking fool.

That nigga probably would kill me with his fucking bare hands if he ever found out some shit like that. Besides, I wasn't ready to be nobody's daddy anyway. I knew that she was better off with a daddy like Mike, rather than a muthafucka who only cared about himself like me. No matter how much I resented the pussy my homie had become, I knew that he still deserved the truth. I just wasn't about to be the nigga to give it to him.

Mike looked at me after touching the picture and then smiled with an eerie expression on his face. Something in his eyes was different, but I couldn't quite put my finger on it.

"Maine bruh, I know everything you saying true Dee. That bitch play with my mind so fucking much sometimes I don't even know who the fuck I am. I love that girl with all of me and she treat me like shit. I'm scared sometimes fool...scared of what I might do to the bitch. Sometimes I get like this when my rage and anger is so strong I can't feel nothing. On the inside I'm still screaming and going the fuck off. However, it's so intense I can't register the emotions. This an insane type of love/hate bruh and I hope you never experience this shit." Mike said as he reached into the center console to get his ID and a bag of weed.

I just looked at him with a puzzled expression on my face as I tried to figure out what the fuck was wrong with him. I wished like a muthafucka I would have brought my gun because Mike was acting like a real fucking lunatic. I had to play that shit off so I wouldn't trigger that nigga's rage again, but I didn't know what to say to some shit like that. Mike saw that I didn't know how to react to what he had said so he laughed and nodded his head instead.

"I know you don't ever want to think about being fucked up like this...its straight bruh. I'm fina get my mind right and I'll be aite. You want a beer or some out this muthafucka? Roll this dope up while I'm gone." Mike said to me as he threw the bag of Kush in my lap.

I was ready to go home and get away from that fucking maniac, or at least get my gun in my hand, but my greed was like hell no. I had to smoke some of his Kush, knowing I didn't have anymore at home. Like a greedy ass nigga, I told Mike to get me an IceHouse and began breaking down the cigar to roll up as he went into the store.

As soon as I saw him disappear into the store, I got my cell out of my pocket and texted LiLi. I had to let her dumb ass know how crazy that maine was at that moment and find out why she kept fucking with him.

"LiLi bruh u kno u wrong. This maine actin like a total psycho. Why you keep fuckin wit his head?"

I watched the door of the store as I rolled up and waited on LiLi to reply back to my text. Just as I was licking the last end of the blunt, my notification went off alerting me that LiLi had texted me back. I damn near punched the dashboard after I read her text.

"Don't you worry about that daddy, Mike aite. I got mine, don't you worry about that. All you do is provide the dick when I need it and keep all that commentary."

I couldn't believe that bitch was trying to play me like she did Mike, brushing me off and telling me to stay in my place. She had me so fucked up. She knew that I wasn't the pussy for her that Mike had grown to be. I'd smack the shit out of her for all that loose lip shit and she knew it. She had to be with some nigga to be talking reckless like that.

I felt a twinge of jealousy and anger burn in my chest when I thought about LiLi being with some other nigga as she texted me talking smart and shit. I imagined her and the nigga sitting there laughing at me as she told him I was another weak ass nigga she had under her spell. That shit made me mad as hell the more I thought about it. That bitch wasn't going to play me too. I'd quit fucking with her funky ass. I should have done that a long time ago anyway, but that pussy was like crack... It just kept calling me, calling me! I shook off those pussy feelings and let the anger inside me take control as I started to text LiLi back. Just as I was typing my second word, another text came through from her. I quickly read it as I continued to watch the door.

"I didn't mean any disrespect with that statement daddy. I said that to show you that you are in total control. I may be with him, but I think about you. I need you. At the end of the day, you are the one I love Dee. Promise I can have you forever...or at least for the night. Tonight at 12 maybe...at our spot. Puddy will be waiting daddy."

Just like that she had me caught up again. I felt excitement and a deep lust start to brew in my groin and creep up through my stomach, and into my heart. I knew that LiLi was running game on me, the same game I'd seen her run on Mike and other niggas. I just couldn't resist it. That animal attraction to her sexy ass was way stronger than my ability to think logically. Little Dee between my legs said fuck all logic get yo girl, take her in yo arms, and fuck her right in the pussy. Fuck Mike's feelings and anybody else's. That's exactly what I planned on doing.

I had a huge grin on my face as I texted LiLi back and let her know I'd be there. Just then Mike walked out of the store with a 12-pack and a pack of blunt wraps in his hand. He still had that suppressed psycho look in his eyes that made the hair on the back of my neck stand up, but I ignored that shit. I had a mission for the night with LiLi so I was about to get full on Mike and then go make love to his bitch...my bitch, or more appropriately our bitch!

Part 3

A Killer Is Born!

Chapter 7

<u>Mike</u>

After dropping Dee off at home, I drove towards my house with a cloud of anguish and anxiety hovering over me. Deep inside that rational side of me that wanted a family and to be happy urged me to believe those bullshit lines LiLi feed me. However, the part of me that knew history was repeating itself reminded me of all the times she had done the same bullshit before. I didn't want to believe the lies anymore just to keep the peace and keep her at home with me and the kids. I was tired of pacifying her lying ass when the kids and I were the ones who ended up being hurt. No, I wasn't going to avoid a verbal confrontation with her anymore. It was time to put everything out on the table and demand that she tell me everything.

I went over what I would say to LiLi in my mind as I drove towards our house. Suddenly, I got the overwhelming feeling that someone was following me. I looked in my rearview mirror to see a black Ford F150 with monster tires following close behind me. I tried to see who was driving, but it was dark and the windshield had tint on the top half. I shrugged and accelerated as I kept my eyes on the road while glancing back at the truck. When I sped up, I noticed the truck did too, and that shit kind of spooked me. Who the fuck was this nigga following me like I was his bitch?

At that moment I wished I would have brought my gun because the muthafucka following me was acting like the robbers, trailing me all close and shit. I tried to keep my eyes on the road ahead of me, but the truck was so fucking close to me I could feel it pushing me down the street. Suddenly, it hit me so hard from the back that I flew forward into the intersection of Winchester and Tchulahoma and began spinning wildly. When I finished spinning, I looked to the side to see a semi-truck plowing towards me. I tried to remain calm and crank my truck back up without shitting on myself, but that wasn't working.

My hands shook uncontrollably as I turned the key repeatedly, but the truck wouldn't start. I cried like a bitch and asked God to save me as the big truck got closer and closer. Just as the semi closed in on me, I turned the key and my truck magically came to life. I punched the gas fast and shot out of the intersection back the way I came as

I thanked God for saving me. I searched the cars sitting at the light, looking for that muthafucka in the black F150, but he was long gone. I would have killed that pussy on sight if he were still on the scene.

I had to sit in McDonald's lot for a few minutes to compose myself before continuing home. That near death experience had my ass shook. My mind was filled with so many thoughts I couldn't concentrate on shit. Who was the muthafucka trying to kill me? Was it Rozel's bitch ass? Or some other nigga LiLi was fucking? I didn't know who the fuck it was. All I knew was I had to stay strapped and ready from then on. No more loafing and thinking I was still living in that fairy tale world I had made up. I had to watch my surroundings and that bitch I laid up with.

For some reason I couldn't get over the feeling that everything was happening because of

LiLi. It was her bringing drama to our relationship because more than likely she was cheating and running around town being a hoe again. Just like I thought history was repeating itself. LiLi hadn't changed a bit and all along I knew she probably never would.

I knew when I got with her she had a deep, sexual sickness due to the abuse she suffered as a kid. I knew that she needed sex all the time and not just sex, but that abusive, hard, dominating sex. I knew all of that bullshit from the jump, but I thought I could change her. I thought love could conquer all and I could give LiLi all of the sex and love that she needed. I was fooling myself from the start.

I couldn't change her and love didn't mean shit to her because she never learned how to give or receive love. I had to face that fucking fact, but it was much easier said than done.

"You gotta learn to let her go Mike." I said to myself as I looked into the rearview mirror and a tear fell from my eye.

I knew what I was supposed to do...what would be best, but I never thought I'd be able to do it. Death was the only thing I thought would take me away from LiLi or her from me. I loved her too much to let her go forever, maybe just long enough for her to get herself together, but not forever.

I wiped the tear from the corner of my eye as I pulled into my driveway and noticed that LiLi's car was gone. That rage I felt before my near death experience came back to me instantly as I got out of my truck and stormed into the house.

"LiLi, where the fuck you at?" I yelled as I stormed into the living room and walked right into Tasha.

That ugly, freaky, red bitch stood there in front of me smirking as she sucked her teeth and looked me up and down. Her yamp ass always tried to fuck with me when LiLi wasn't around, but when LiLi was there she talked down on me and urged her to leave me. That was just because that bitch wanted me for herself. She had me fucked up though because she wasn't my type. She was way too ratchet for me and I didn't fuck with friends. That was one of my golden rules...you never fuck with your mate's friend. That was a major no-no in my book and I resented Tasha's maggot ass even more for constantly trying me.

"Umm sexy. LiLi funky ass gone. She had to run to the store for a minute, but why don't you gone let me suck you up before she gets back." Tasha said licking her lips as she stepped closer to me.

I almost vomited in my mouth watching Tasha try to seduce me by licking her lips and rubbing herself. I trembled with anger and clenched my fists as my rage continued to build inside. I almost put that hoe's head through the wall as she put her arms around my neck and I mushed her the fuck away from me.

"Maine, ole nasty ass bitch, have you lost yo fucking mind? I would never fuck something like you. So get yo little dirty ass kids and take yo hot, soggy, rancid pussy ass on out of my house....NOW BITCH!" I yelled so loud I felt the words vibrate through my body.

Tasha knew I wasn't bullshitting from the look in my eyes, so she quickly gathered her kids, her hair products, and got the fuck out of my house.

"I hope LiLi leave yo weak ass. You ain't shit but a pussy. She got more heart than you because she sho do her thang and don't give a fuck about you catching her...ahhhhh PUSSY!" Tasha yelled as she walked out of my door and I slammed it behind her.

The words Tasha spewed at me like daggers pierced my heart and played over and over again in my head. I knew everything she said about LiLi was true. If anyone would know what LiLi was doing, it would be her. But could I trust the word of a hoe who wanted to fuck me? I didn't know what to think as I stormed through the house looking for my kids. After checking everywhere I figured LiLi had dropped them off to my mother so I went into the living room to sit on the couch as I called to confirm.

After talking to my mother and she told me LiLi had dropped the kids off a couple of hours earlier, I hung up knowing that my kids were okay. I was relieved my kids were safe and wouldn't be at home to hear what would happen when their mama got home. However, I was also mad as hell knowing that LiLi had left as soon as I did, taking my kids to my mama so she could go fuck off. She had me so fucked up.

I raged into our bedroom with hate in my eyes, throwing clothes and flipping furniture. Tears fell from my eyes and I felt out of control as I cursed at the lying bitch who wasn't there. I made my way into our closet and began to pull down all of the expensive dresses and purses LiLi always had me buy, ripping them and throwing them in a pile on the floor. I was acting like a real bitch having a tantrum as I knocked down all of the boxes at the top of her side of the closet.

Just then something heavy fell from the shelf and I heard it make a loud clink noise as it tapped the buckle on one of LiLi's shoes. I bent down and picked up the huge beer mug that had fallen and sucked my teeth as I read the words written on it. There in red letters was the phrase "Pure Passion Loves Its Employees" written on the side of the mug. I couldn't understand why the hell LiLi had a Pure Passion employee mug. That discovery triggered my curiosity and for the first time since I had come home from doing that bid, I did a full search of our bedroom.

I went around the room so fast and with such fury it looked as if a tornado had hit when I was done. When it was all over, I sat on the edge of the bed with my head in my hands, wishing I had never searched for anything. I wished I had never found the duffle bag full of dance clothes, the hotel towels, the box of condoms, and mysterious bank statement. I wished I could take everything back and go back to the pussy, oblivious nigga I had been at least I was happy then and didn't feel like I was losing my damn mind. Hell, ignorance was bliss for me, so maybe I was better off not knowing. It was too late for not knowing by then though. I had to face the fact that LiLi was not who I wanted her to be and I was not important to her.

That was a very hard pill to swallow after giving her so much of me. I gave her more of myself that I even knew was possible. For over seven years, the sun rose and set in LiLi's ass...everything I did was for her. I thought of her before I thought of myself. I gave up so much just to be with her and make sure she was safe. She was the one who came from an abusive home with her nasty, perverted aunt. She was the one running away, stealing, and eating out of garbage cans.

I had a home and a family. My mother was always there for me and made sure I had everything that I needed. My mother showed me what a strong black woman looked like and that's why I always valued LiLi so much. I tried to make LiLi the woman my mother had always been and that was my first mistake. I couldn't change her and I should have never tried, but I did. I did, and look where it got me.

"It's time to face the music, Mike. It's time to hear the truth no matter how ugly it may be." I said to myself as I sat on my bed and stared at myself in the mirror.

It was time for me to hear the truth, whatever it was. I just hoped I could keep my shit together when I did. I hoped I would be able to control myself, and not do something I would regret. Only time would tell though.

I closed my eyes and held my chin in my hands as I leaned forward in the bed and waited on LiLi to come home. I had to wonder as I sat there, would the next few hours prove that LiLi really loved me and we had a viable future together? Or would LiLi's actions break me down and help give birth to a killer?

Chapter 8

LiLi

I rushed to the house as fast as I could, pushing my Chrysler 300 to the dash. However, it was all in vain. When I pulled on the street, my fucking heart dropped when I saw Mike's truck already in the yard. He had beat me to the house and he knew the kids were gone already. All hell was about to break loose. I knew Mike was about to act a fool as soon as I stepped into the house, so I tried to prepare myself.

I pulled into the driveway behind Mike's truck, partially in the street. I wanted to leave myself a good escape route just in case that nigga acted crazy when I got inside. Once I cut my car off, I took a Lortab out of my purse and swallowed it down with the Calypso watermelon juice I was drinking as I grabbed my Kush blunt out of the ashtray. I was going to get faded in order to face Mike and all the anger he was about to throw at me. I lit the blunt and inhaled the Kush smoke as I stared upstairs at our bedroom window. Everything was still and dark inside. I would have thought no one was home if Mike's truck wasn't in the yard.

The house looked eerily quiet from the outside as I sat there trembling, afraid to go inside. A part of me wanted to just pull the fuck off and never come back, but I knew I couldn't do that. I couldn't just up and leave my kids, Mike, and the only world I knew. What would I do on my own without Mike taking care of the bills and making sure everything was alright? No matter how much I loved my freedom and claimed to be independent, I knew that deep down I needed Mike. Who else would put up with my dog ass and still remain a good man?

I took my final hit of the blunt before ashing it. I held in the thick cloud of Kush smoke as I closed my eyes and sat back in my seat to let the THC take its effect. I felt so calm and serene in that moment, safe and sound in my car closed off from the world. I wanted to stay there forever and avoid the terrible scene that would happen when I faced Mike. In a perfect world, I would have been able to use a magical remote to fast forward right pass the entire spectacle and the whole fucked up nightmare my life had become. Only if the world was perfect, however it wasn't.

If the world was perfect, I wouldn't have lost my parents in a car accident when I was five, taken by a fucking drunk driver. If the world were perfect, I wouldn't have been left with an aunt who resented my existence and used me for her own sexual and sadistic gratification. If the world were perfect, I wouldn't have wished for someone to love me when I had no one and when that someone never came I wouldn't have wished to die. No, the world was never perfect for me and probably never would be. It was like I was cursed from that day my parents were taken from me. Facing the fact that my life would never be what I really wanted it to be was a harsh reality, but I had to face that fact.

Fucked up shit always happened to me because I deserved it. I was cursed and I deserved every bad fucking thing that happened to me...at least that's what I told myself. It was easier that way. When I was little and being raped and beaten every day, I told myself that I deserved all of the bad shit that happened to me and that's why no one ever helped me. I believed I deserved the bad; therefore, it couldn't hurt me to do bad and inflict the pain I felt on others. That's why I wouldn't allow myself to give a fuck. Why should I? In the end, I would have a fucked up ending, so who cares how I got there.

I told myself that for so long I began to believe it...live it. Now it just comes natural..I would hurt others because I hurt so badly. I didn't really want to though. I just did fucked up shit and I had no idea how to change it. I didn't even know if I really wanted to change it. It was easier not giving a fuck or having to face those demons of the past.

Tears fell from my eyes as I thought about the happier times I had with Mike. I wondered why I couldn't be that LiLi I used to be all of the time. Why did I have to fuck up everything good in my life?

"You're a bad seed nobody wants, that's why." I told myself as I looked into the rearview mirror and tears ran down my face.

Those weren't my words; they were the words my aunt told me all of my life. Those were the words imprinted in my brain and my heart that drove me to do every fucked up thing I did.

Thinking about my aunt made anger flicker in my heart and a deep anxiety start to consume me. I hated remembering the hell I lived with her. I wiped away my tears with the back of my hand and stared up at the window one more time before stepping out of the car.

"Nothing can hurt you worse than she did LiLi. Your life is what it is. Either Mike will stay or go, who gives a fuck. Everyone leaves anyway...no one wants you. Just face this shit and then get back to getting what you need. Love is not in the cards for you." I said out loud to myself as I walked up on the porch and into the house.

When I stepped inside of the house, it was unusually quiet, so still. I looked around for Mike downstairs, creeping through the darkness not making a sound. I felt as if I was suffocating as I stealthed around the hot, stuffy house and anxiety crept through my body. It was late July in

Memphis and even though it was after eight at night it was still very hot, which made me wonder why Mike didn't have the air on. Mike hated to sweat and he hated for our house to be humid and stuffy, so I knew something bad was brewing as I crept through the house inhaling the stifling air.

I made my way to the bottom of the stairwell and stared up into the darkness, holding my breath. My hand shook as I grabbed the banister and began creeping up the stairs, trying not to make a sound. I couldn't remember ever being as scared of Mike as I was at that moment. I could feel his anger and hurt burning through my skin as I stepped up on to the landing and looked into our bedroom door.

I focused my eyes and peered through the darkness to see Mike sitting on the bed with shit all around him. I noticed one of my red bottom shoes in the hallway as I crept closer, so I quickly picked it up and stepped forward to flick on the light in our room. When the light illuminated the darkness all around me, I almost fainted from the sight of my room. Everything inside was destroyed, damaged, or thrown around like trash. Mike had gone completely crazy ripping my clothes, flipping the dressers, and putting his foot through our 46 inch plasma TV.

At that moment all of the fear and anxiety I felt inside was replaced by pure rage. How dare he break everything we owned because he had a fucking temper tantrum like a child. I had helped get most of that shit with my money and he had no right to destroy shit just because things wasn't going his way. Hell naw, he had me so fucked up. Before I knew it, I was in Mike's face yelling and cursing as he sat there in a trance, not moving just staring at me with a blank expression.

If I wasn't so fucking blinded by anger over him destroying the room, I would have noticed how angry he was and maybe I could have avoided what happened next. However just like an angry black woman, I continued to go off, mushing Mike in his head and taunting him.

"Mike, what the fuck is wrong with you? Have you lost yo muthafucking mind in here tearing up my shit? Nigga, I bought most of this shit. Some of them outfits cost more than yo broke ass will make in a year. You got me so fucked up. Yo bitch ass about to pay for a new TV, some more shoes, and you replacing my fucking dresses. You do not get to act like a fucking child when yo feelings hurt. All this pussy shit is disgusting. What do you have to say for yourself, you fucking psycho? Huh? You hear me muthafucka....WHAT THE FUCK IS WRONG WITH YOU MIKKKEE!" I yelled in Mike's face as I bent over with my hands on my hips.

132

I watched as his hands begin to tremble and he bit his lip. I could see a rage in his eyes that gave me a sick feeling in the pit of my stomach. The hair on the back of my neck and arms stood up as Mike suddenly looked me directly in the eyes. He was physically there on the bed before me, but the look in his eyes told me he wasn't home. He had lost his mind for real and I knew I had to get the fuck away from him right then.

I slowly stood up while holding my breath and took a step back towards the bathroom door. Just then Mike jumped up so fast, he caught me off guard as he wrapped his hands around my neck, picking me up in the air.

"What's wrong with me? You wonna know what's wrong with me, LiLi? You are what the fuck is wrong with me. Bitch, you drive me crazy trying to play with my emotions and use me as your own personal cake boy. You act like you love me when it's convenient for you, but other than that you treat me like shit. I deserve better than this LiLi. I deserve a bitch who will tell me the truth. TELL ME THE TRUTH, LILI!" Mike yelled as he shook me violently in the air like a rag doll.

I felt my teeth chatter and my eyes rolled in the back of my head as Mike squeezed my neck and continued to choke me as he yelled.

"Tell me LiLi. Why do you have a dance bag with nasty clothes and condoms and shit in it? Why did I find a receipt from another bank account with over $30,000 in it, but I'm living check-to-check to pay our bills? Where do you work LiLi? Who the fuck are you?" Mike yelled at me as I clawed at his hands, trying to get him to release his grip on my throat.

I could feel the air and life seeping out of me with the more pressure Mike put on my neck. I knew I was about to pass out and I didn't want to. I just wanted him to leave me the fuck alone and let me fucking go. I kicked, squirmed, and continued to claw at Mike's hand, trying to get him to let me go. Tears ran from my eyes and I felt as if I would pee on myself as the room began to spin.

Suddenly, Mike released his grip on my throat and threw me on to the bed where I lay there gasping and crying. I couldn't believe Mike had put his hands on me. Although I liked a little violence mixed in with my sex or the occasional dominating smack, that insane rage I saw in Mike's eyes at that moment was not okay. I was totally afraid of him and what he was capable of. All I wanted to do was get away from him.

"LiLi baby, I'm sorry for hurting you. You deserve it though because you keep lying. Tell me, baby. Answer my questions, LiLi, and I promise I won't get mad. I just need to know. LiLi please, you owe me that much." Mike said pleading with me as he walked over to the bed and got on his knees in front of me.

Tears rolled down his face as he stared at me with that insane look and begged me to tell him the truth. I swallowed down the lump in my sore, dry throat, and wiped away my tears as I stared into Mike's eyes. I saw all of the hurt and pain I had caused him over the years as he begged me to tell him what he wanted to know.

"LiLi, please talk to me. Tell me the truth that's all I want." Mike said pleading with me again.

I knew I had to tell him the truth about my job, but I was so afraid of the consequences. I had to tell him on my own fucking terms. I was not giving him the opportunity to wrap his big ass hands around my neck again. I rubbed Mike's head gently as I scooted to the edge of the bed and stood up. Mike was so busy crying and mumbling to himself he didn't even notice I was up off the bed until I was halfway to the bathroom.

"LiLi, where the fuck you going, maine?" I heard Mike yell as I ran into the bathroom with my purse in my hand and locked the door.

My heart raced like a herd of wild horses as Mike beat on the bathroom door and demanded I let him in and tell him the truth.

"LiLi bitch, you think this a muthafucking game. Tell me what you do every day. TELL ME!!" Mike yelled over and over again, driving me insane as his voice echoed through the door.

I covered my ears with my hands and slid down the door as he continued to hit and bang while yelling for me to tell him. The whole scene was fucking crazy like something out of a soap opera. All I wanted at that moment was for it all to end, so I could go back to living the way I was before. I figured telling Mike the truth couldn't hurt him any more than he already was so I bit my bottom lip before spilling the beans.

"I'm a stripper Mike...you happy now. I quit that lame ass job you helped me get about 8 months ago. Since then, I have been working at Pure Passion, getting my bank up. That $30,000 is what I have made in 8 months. I'm sorry Mike, but you knew how I was from the start. I can't be the female you want me to be… I'm LiLi and not your mother. Take me or leave me...I'm a stripper MIKE!" I yelled through the door, releasing all of the pinned up fear, anger, and anxiety I felt.

For a few seconds I felt better having told Mike a piece of the truth. However, after a few seconds of a dead, eerie silence, I quickly began to regret telling him anything.

"Mike….Mike are you out there? I'm sorry Mike, do you forgive me?" I asked through the door as I turned to kneel at the door and peep out of the key hole.

When I put my eye to the hole, I could see Mike coming out of the closet with his gun safe in his hands. Panic rushed over me in quick, forceful waves, telling me that things were about to get ugly. Instinctually, I went into my purse to get my phone and dialed Dee's number as I got up off the floor with the Bambi legs and got into the tub. I didn't want him to shoot through the door and kill me, so I laid down in the giant, whirlpool tub as I waited for Dee to answer his phone.

It felt like an eternity laying there in the tub waiting on Dee to answer the phone as I watched the handle of the door. I still couldn't hear a sound coming from the bedroom, but I knew Mike's crazy ass was still out there just waiting on me to come out. I knew that if I did go out he would kill me for sure before turning the gun on himself, and I was not about to let that happen.

I would stay in there all damn night if I had to, but I hoped Dee would come to my rescue. I needed him to come rescue me because I couldn't call the police. That's not how we handled domestic situations like that by calling the police because eventually we would always get back together. However, I wondered would we be able to repair the shards of our shattered relationship after a breakdown like this one.

I continued to think of the 'what if's' until I heard Dee answer his phone, laughing and coughing as he hit a blunt. Before he could get hello out of his mouth good, I began to cry and beg him to help me.

"Please Dee, you have to come. Mike has went crazy. He found my dance clothes and secret bank account. After that the psycho tore up everything, he choked me out to the point I felt like I was going to die, but I was able to slip away into the bathroom. I'm in the bathroom now hiding while his crazy ass out there getting his gun out of the safe. You have to come help me, daddy. He's your friend; he'll listen to you. He's going to kill me though. Help me, Dee, please." I whispered as tears ran down my cheeks.

I was so scared at that moment I almost jumped out of my skin when Mike suddenly began to beat on and kick the door again.

"LiLi bitch, I'ma kill you...bitch you nasty as hell. I'm sitting up here fucking you raw and kissing you and yo yamp ass out here stripping. Why LiLi? Why?" Mike yelled crying as he tried to knock the bathroom door down.

I was convinced his big ass would knock it down eventually and drag me out by my hair, so I had to get Dee to come.

"Dee, please help me. You can't let him kill me. What would happen to our daughter and the other kids if he killed me and he ended up in jail? You'd have to take them all then and tell them what happened." I said to Dee through my tears as my hands shook.

I was going to try reverse psychology and anything else I could to get him to help. I needed someone to save me from Mike's wrath and I knew the best person to do that would be his best friend.

"Just stay in there LiLi, I'm on my way...I'm right down the street in south Memphis. I'm com..." Dee said to me as my phone cut off and I broke down, listening to Mike beat on the bathroom door with his gun.

Chapter 9

Dee

I hung up the phone shaking my head as LiLi's phone cut off. I felt a chill run through my body as I remembered the sound of LiLi crying into the phone as Mike raged in the background. That shit really got to me and had me feeling like something really bad was about to happen. Up until that point, I was out having a good time with this lil' bitch I had just met, and then LiLi called, stopping everything I had planned.

I was going to ignore her call at first, but when I saw that she was going to keep letting the phone ring I had to answer. Mike was going crazy in the background, threatening to kill her and then himself as she cried and whispered into the phone. I couldn't even imagine what they were into it for, but I hoped it wasn't about me as I turned my car

144

around and headed back to the house of the female I had with me.

I was scared as shit of Mike when he was all crazy and shit, but I couldn't leave LiLi to deal with that nigga and his rage all by herself. I knew I had to go over there and try to talk Mike's crazy ass down. I didn't want neither one of their blood on my hands and wasn't no way in hell I was taking nobody's kids in if they asses died. The best thing for me to do was to try to defuse the situation and get LiLi away from Mike's crazy ass for good.

"What's going on?" The light skinned girl in my passenger seat asked me as I pulled back into her apartments.

I almost forgot that bitch was even sitting there next to me because I was so wrapped up in my thoughts. I knew she had to be irritated as fuck seeing how quickly my mood had changed after I got a phone call from another female. I didn't give a fuck though because she meant nothing to me. I was just about to get a quick fuck in and drop her ass back off anyway, not wife her. Hell, I couldn't even remember the bitch's name as I pulled in front of her apartment to let her out.

"Oh I'm sorry, lil' mama. I got a family emergency. We gotta postpone this shit until another day. I'll call you though when I get a chance." I said to the girl as I glared impatiently from her to the door handle, urging her to get the fuck out.

I guess my urgency rubbed the girl the wrong way because I saw attitude quickly surge through her body as she rolled her eyes and sucked her teeth. I knew she had heard LiLi's voice on the other end of my phone, but I didn't give a fuck. She wasn't my bitch and neither was LiLi, but I did have more loyalty to LiLi. This girl was just a lil' fuck junt I picked up in the hood and was about to burn her dome up, nothing more...nothing less. Now she was sitting her long head ass in my car like she wasn't going to get out as my bitch waited on me to save her. Her little pelican looking ass had to go and fast. I reached over and opened the door before unhooking her seat belt and looking at her.

"Nigga please, that wasn't no family emergency. That was some bitch calling you and shit. You ain't all that ole hoe ass boy. You think you gonna pick me up then brush me off when some bitch call. I'm not going no fucking where. You said we was going to Applebee's and I'm not getting out until we do." The chick said as she folded her arms, refusing to get out.

That bitch had the right nigga at the wrong moment. Before she could even blink, I had reached over and mushed that bitch by her head so hard that she flew out of my car and hit the ground.

I quickly scooted into the passenger seat, closed and locked my passenger door, and sped out of the lot as the girl cursed and ran behind my car. She threw rocks at my back window trying to break it as I turned the corner and left her apartments.

I heard my back passenger window crack as I got on the main strip only to look back and see that one of the rocks she threw had put a small hole in the glass. I wanted to go back and whoop her ass then. She was lucky I had more pressing matters at the moment or I would have went to get my little sister to drag her for me.

I cursed as I drove to my house and got my gun to go save LiLi. I jumped on the e-way going 90 mph, flying to the Haven and straight into the chaotic scene LiLi had created. When I got to LiLi and Mike's house, I parked on the street, checking my gun and sticking my extra clip in the pocket on my cargo jogging pants. I walked up to the house with my gun in my hand, breathing hard with each step. Adrenaline surged through my body making me feel like I would pass out as I scanned the windows for lights or any type of movement. There were no lights on in the house and I didn't see anyone in any of the windows as I got closer. I felt like I was a fucking cowboy in a western movie, going to meet my opponent for a duel to the death.

The last thing I wanted to do was end up in a standoff with my best friend, or worse have to kill him. However, I was prepared to do what I had to do. Although I was scared shitless at the thought of facing the beast that Mike had become, I would if I had to. I just hoped I would be able to get in there and calm him down without anyone getting hurt.

My legs trembled as I stepped up on the porch and I could hear Mike yelling and raging inside. He sounded like a complete monster as he demanded LiLi to open the door and meet her death. I almost ran the fuck away when his voice got louder and deeper, sending chills all through my body. I wasn't no bitch, but I think anybody, man or woman, would have been scared if they heard the untamed, sadistic rage that was in Mike's voice. I wasn't sure I would be able to calm him down as I turned the doorknob and entered the house.

It was hot and dark inside of Mike and LiLi's house when I entered, which was two things I was not used to it being. Their house was usually filled with kids running and playing and the smells of homemade food Mike's mama had come over and cooked along with some type of music playing. It was always cool and refreshing when you stepped into their house…it just felt like a home. It didn't feel like that when I entered that time. All I could feel as I slowly walked up the stairs was the hate and hurt Mike felt and the nagging fear in my heart.

Mike's voice continued to vibrate through my body as I got half way up the steps. I could hear LiLi crying at that point, begging Mike just to go and telling him how sorry she was. I hated the fact that her sexual yearning had led to the dire situation she was now in, but I wondered was that exactly what she needed to leave Mike for good and change her ways. Maybe this would be what she needed to push her away from Mike and straight to me, to be the good bitch I knew she could be.

Thoughts of possibly getting LiLi and living a happy life with her filled my mind giving me strength as I approached the top of the steps. I checked my gun and held it down to my side as Mike came into view. He looked like a fucking werewolf with rabies as his big, black, bald-headed ass stood in front of the bathroom door with his gun in his hand. I watched Mike unleash a combination of kicks and punches to the door while cursing as I walked on to the landing, trembling with fear.

Just as I got to the door and was about to creep into the room to get an advantage point on Mike, he turned towards me quickly with his gun drawn. I just knew he had shot me in the face as he squeezed off a round that whizzed right by my head. I could tell he didn't intend to do it though because as soon as he did he laid his gun on the dresser and walked towards me with his hands up.

"Maine bruh, I promise I didn't mean to do that shit. You my nigga I would never fucking kill you.....but this Bitch got me Fucked UP!" Mike yelled walking towards me with his arms still in the air before abruptly stopping and running back to the door to bang on it and yell.

"LiLi open this fucking door. I promise I'm calm now. Maine open the muthafucking door before I shoot through the muthafucka. Come out here and talk to me LiLi." Mike begged as I stood there with my gun still in my hand dazed at the fucking spectacle unfolding in front of me.

I didn't know whether I should have ran or what as I watched Mike go crazy, banging on the door while screaming, hysterically. I couldn't run and leave LiLi with the maniac. I knew I had to get Mike to calm the fuck down, but I wasn't a fool. I wouldn't put my gun down no matter what happened. I tucked my right hand holding my gun behind my back as I walked towards Mike with my left hand out. I was going to have to talk him down like you would do a terrorist.

"Mike, come on my nigga. We talked about this bruh...she ain't worth it. Ain't no female worth it, bruh. Look at yourself my nigga. You off yo muthafucking rocker behind some shit she may or may not be doing, bruhhh. You better than this my nigga. Calm the fuck down." I said to Mike as I got closer to him and took the gun he had picked back up out of his hand.

I sat Mike's gun back on the dresser next to the bathroom door as he stood there frozen just staring at me with tears and snot running down his face. On one hand I felt sorry for my nigga going through so much pain and turmoil at the hands of an evil bitch who only cared about herself. On the other hand I didn't give two fucks about his feelings. That nigga was crazy as hell and didn't deserve a bad bitch like LiLi. I saw her first anyway. She was supposed to been mine all along, yet there Mike was abusing the privilege of having that fine bitch all of the time. I deserved that.

I deserved a good bitch to fuck me right and take care of home while I ran the streets and did my thang. I wasn't ready to be all tied down like a fucking family man, but I was willing to get a main bitch and LiLi could be the perfect main bitch with a little work. I just had to get her away from Mike's crazy ass first. I had to break the spell they had on each other and get LiLi where I wanted her to be. I'd be happy then and they probably would too. At the rate they were going, someone was sure to end up dead eventually.

Mike grabbed my arm as I helped him sit down on the chest at the foot of their bed. Just then LiLi yelled out my name and I almost ran to the door. I could hear the desperation in her voice as she called out to me over and over again. I wanted to say something, but the look on Mike's face told me not to say shit.

"Mike, you alright bruh. Stay calm. Y'all gotta talk this shit out. I'ma get her out of the bathroom and y'all gonna talk. Okay?" I asked

Mike as he shook his head up and down while staring into space.

It felt like I was in the fucking Twilight Zone watching that nigga sit there looking like a zombie. I wanted to get the fuck out of that house fast. I walked over to the bathroom door, turning around a couple of times to look back at Mike. He was still sitting there when I turned around the last time, but he looked calmer and more mentally stable as he met my eyes and shook his head. I took that as a good sign, so I yelled for LiLi to come out as I stepped back away from the door. After confirming it was me, I heard LiLi unlike the door and move something heavy she had slid in front of it.

She ran out of the bathroom and straight into my arms, catching me off guard. I didn't know what to do with LiLi all over me and Mike sitting on the chest staring at us with a puzzled look. I couldn't believe I had managed to calm that raging animal and get LiLi out only to have her fuck it up. I knew I had to get us out of the house safely, so Mike could work through his feelings alone. I just had to make LiLi realize it was not the time for her to thank me not in front of the crazy ass nigga I had just stopped from killing her.

I quickly pushed LiLi away from me and stared at her with a serious look on my face as Mike continued to look on. LiLi cried and yelled that Mike was crazy as she tried to hold on to me again. I wanted no parts of comforting her ass at that moment. Hell, I didn't want to be there at all. I tried to shake LiLi off like we were playing football, but she grabbed my arm and held on.

I turned to look at Mike like 'nigga get yo bitch' as LiLi continued to cry and hold my arm. Just then he stood up yelling causing LiLi to shut the fuck up instantly and let go of my arm.

"Shut the fuck up LiLi. Dee, I appreciate you coming over here to help me out, but I think me and my girl got it from here." Mike said with an angry look on his face as he walked slowly towards the dresser I had sat his gun back on.

I didn't know what to do at that moment as LiLi stepped behind me and Mike walked closer to his gun.

"By the way, homeboy, how did you know to come over here just now?" Mike asked me calmly as he inched closer to his gun.

I couldn't say shit as I stood there shaking. My mouth was dry as fuck and my throat seemed to be closing up. All I could do was think about the bullet I may have to put in my homie's head. Time seemed to stand still at that moment, nothing existed but me and my gun. I was in a fucking zone, so much so I didn't even hear Mike as he yelled the question again.

"How the FUCK did you know to come over here, Dee?" Mike yelled as he put his gun on the dresser and prepared to grab his gun.

I slowly lifted my arm to reveal I was still carrying my gun as I heard LiLi's voice.

"I called him Mike. I called him to save me from you." LiLi yelled out of spite, sending our already volatile situation into a tailspin of chaos and pain.

All I could do was quickly glance at LiLi with a 'what the fuck look' on my face before I heard the first shot from Mike's gun. I turned back around to see him standing in the bathroom door crying as we both let go of one shot in each other's direction.

More titles by True Glory Publishing……..

By Niki Jilvontae:

A Broken Girl's Journey

http://www.amazon.com/BROKEN-GIRLS-JOURNEY-Niki-Jilvontae-ebook/dp/B00IICJRQK/ref=sr_1_5?ie=UTF8&qid=141341 9382&sr=8-5&keywords=niki+jilvontae

A Broken Girl's Journey 2

http://www.amazon.com/BROKEN-GIRLS-JOURNEY-ebook/dp/B00J9ZM9YW/ref=sr_1_4?ie=UTF8&qid=1413 419382&sr=8-4&keywords=niki+jilvontae

A Broken Girl's Journey 3

http://www.amazon.com/BROKEN-GIRLS-JOURNEY-ebook/dp/B00JVDFTBM/ref=sr_1_1?ie=UTF8&qid=1413 419382&sr=8-1&keywords=niki+jilvontae

A Broken Girl's Journey 4: Kylie's Song

http://www.amazon.com/Broken-Girls-Journey-Kylies-Song-

160

ebook/dp/B00NK89604/ref=sr_1_6?ie=UTF8&qid=14134
19382&sr=8-6&keywords=niki+jilvontae

A Long Way from Home

http://www.amazon.com/Long-Way-Home-Niki-Jilvontae-
ebook/dp/B00LCN252U/ref=sr_1_3?ie=UTF8&qid=14134
19382&sr=8-3&keywords=niki+jilvontae

By NyChel Dior:
Deadly Temptation

http://www.amazon.com/DEADLY-TEMPTATION-
NyChel-Dior-
ebook/dp/B00IN9YW36/ref=sr_1_1?s=digital-
text&ie=UTF8&qid=1413418436&sr=1-
1&keywords=DEADLY+TEMPTATION

Deadly Temptation 2-Love's Story
http://www.amazon.com/DEADLY-TEMPTATION-2-
NYCHEL-DIOR-
ebook/dp/B00NF29WUE/ref=cm_cr_pr_pdt_img_top?ie=
UTF8

By KC Blaze

Pleasure of Pain Part 1 Shameek Speight

http://www.amazon.com/Pleasure-pain-Shameek-Speight-ebook/dp/B005C68BE4/ref=sr_1_1?s=digital-text&ie=UTF8&qid=1413593888&sr=1-1&keywords=pleasure+of+pain

Your Husband, My Man Part 2 KC Blaze

http://www.amazon.com/Your-Husband-Man-YOUR-HUSBAND-ebook/dp/B00MUAKRPQ/ref=sr_1_1?ie=UTF8&qid=1413593158&sr=8-1&keywords=your+husband+my+man+2

Your Husband, My Man Part 3 KC Blaze

http://www.amazon.com/Your-Husband-My-Man-3-ebook/dp/B00OJODI8Y/ref=sr_1_1?ie=UTF8&qid=14135 93252&sr=8-1&keywords=your+husband+my+man+3+kc+blaze

By Shameek Speight

Pleasure of Pain Part 1 Shameek Speight

http://www.amazon.com/Pleasure-pain-Shameek-Speight-ebook/dp/B005C68BE4/ref=sr_1_1?s=digital-text&ie=UTF8&qid=1413593888&sr=1-1&keywords=pleasure+of+pain

Child of a Crackhead I Shameek Speight

http://www.amazon.com/CHILD-CRACKHEAD-Part-1-
ebook/dp/B0049U4W56/ref=sr_1_1?s=digital-
text&ie=UTF8&qid=1413594876&sr=1-
1&keywords=child+of+a+crackhead

Child of a Crackhead II Shameek Speight

http://www.amazon.com/CHILD-CRACKHEAD-II-
Shameek-Speight-
ebook/dp/B004MME12K/ref=sr_1_2?ie=UTF8&qid=1413
593375&sr=8-2&keywords=child+of+a+crackhead+series

By Sha Cole

Her Mother's Love Part 1

http://www.amazon.com/Her-Mothers-love-Sha-Cole-
ebook/dp/B00H93Z03I/ref=sr_1_1?s=digital-
text&ie=UTF8&qid=1405463882&sr=1-
1&keywords=her+mothers+love

Her Mother's Love Part 2

http://www.amazon.com/HER-MOTHERS-LOVE-Sha-
Cole-

ebook/dp/B00IKBGWW6/ref=pd_sim_kstore_1?ie=UTF8
&refRID=1EFA9EPXRPBSQPZVWHM0

Her Mother's Love Part 3

http://www.amazon.com/Her-Mothers-Love-Sha-Cole-
ebook/dp/B00L2SHLNI/ref=pd_sim_kstore_1?ie=UTF8&r
efRID=1AW831PBNBGAPPP9G8A9

Made in the USA
Lexington, KY
13 April 2018